THE

WHEEL OF

Doll

Novels by Jonathan Ames

THE

WHEEL OF

JONATHAN AMES

MULHOLLAND BOOKS

LITTLE, BROWN AND COMPANY

NEW YORK BOSTON LONDON

Mulholland Books / Little, Brown and Company
Hachette Book Group
1290 Avenue of the Americas, New York, NY 10104
mulhollandbooks.com

First Edition: September 2022

Mulholland Books is an imprint of Little, Brown and Company, a division of Hachette Book Group, Inc. The Mulholland Books name and logo are trademarks of Hachette Book Group, Inc.

The publisher is not responsible for websites (or their content) that are not owned by the publisher.

The Hachette Speakers Bureau provides a wide range of authors for speaking events. To find out more, go to hachettespeakersbureau.com or call (866) 376-6591.

ISBN 978-0-316-28815-6
LCCN 2022936430

Printing 1 , 2022

LSC-C

Printed in the United States of America

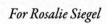

For Rosalie Siegel

PART I

1.

ONE OF MY FLAWS is that I'm a great one for asking questions, but I'm mediocre to poor at answers. Which isn't the best trait for a detective.

Though it may be why, of late, I've become an armchair Buddhist.

In Buddhism, you're meant to question everything, including the idea of questioning everything.

And really there are no *answers,* anyway.

But that's in Nirvana. Which is where you get to go when you become enlightened. I hear it's very peaceful there.

But in this messy realm — the realm of women and men and all their myriad problems — there are *some* answers to *some* questions.

You can figure *some* things out.

Which is why you need detectives. Even mediocre-to-poor ones like me.

Because finding a killer can be like finding an answer.

But I'm getting ahead of myself.

The afternoon when all this began, it seemed like just another nice cold Los Angeles day — and by cold, I mean sixty-five degrees — early in 2020. January 10, 2020, to be exact, a Friday.

It was around 4:40 and I had just left my house and gotten into my car, a 1985 royal-blue Chevy Caprice Classic, once the preferred vehicle for police forces in the twentieth century. Which was a long time ago now, and not just in years.

I started the Caprice and let it warm up a second, since it's an old car like an old man and always needs a moment to gather itself and get its pants on. But despite its age and three hundred thousand miles, it's not ready to die. Very few of us are.

To pass the time, I lit a joint.

Then I took a sip of coffee from my thermos. I'm one of those people — maybe the only one — that lives on coffee and pot and small fish: pickled herring, sardines, and kippers.

As I took a second sip, I put the radio on, which was already tuned to 88.9 — a strange college station, my favorite — and then I took another hit of my joint and another sip of my coffee, and feeling that wonderful alchemy of the cannabis and the caffeine — you're ready to go somewhere but don't care too much if you make it — I backed out of the garage and rolled down my dead-end street, Glen Alder.

I was on my way to my office to meet a potential new client — we had a 5:30 appointment — and I needed the business.

From Glen Alder, I turned right onto Beachwood, and a black Challenger, with tinted windows, parked on the corner, swung in behind me, reckless-like and urgent, and I felt a small tingle of alarm.

Since marijuana doesn't make me paranoid, except when I eat it, I had to assume that the tingle was coming — like a preconscious telegram — from that special part of the brain that knows things before it knows things. But that part of the brain doesn't use words. It uses feelings. Like *foreboding*. And *fear*.

Then again, I told myself, a muscle car like a Challenger isn't great for a tail job — it's too conspicuous and sticks out too much. *So maybe it is the pot,* I thought. *Nobody would follow me in that car.*

Or maybe whoever was in the Challenger didn't care if I spotted them. Maybe they didn't care about being discreet, which could make them cops. Undercover but showing themselves. The undercover units like muscle cars, and so it was worrisome if it was detectives. The LAPD wasn't fond of me. Hadn't been for a while.

I tried to see who was driving the car, but the sun — which was already starting to set — was glinting off the Challenger's windshield, just about blinding me, though I could distinguish that there were two shapes in the front seat.

Which would make sense if they were police. They always travel in pairs.

When I turned left on Franklin, the Challenger turned left, which wasn't so unusual, one goes right or left there, and I told myself to forget about it. Told myself I was being jumpy.

Franklin has four narrow lanes, and I went to the far-right lane, nice and slow, which is often how I drive — senior citizen–like and methodical, because I'm usually smoking a joint, like I was just then, and so I try to be extra careful, giving myself plenty of room for error and delayed marijuana reaction time.

But I also drive slowly because I try, as a fledgling student of Buddhism, to be mindful.

I try to do that thing where when you're driving, you're driving; like when you're washing the dishes, you're washing the dishes.

The result is that between the mindfulness and the marijuana, I'm an annoyingly slow driver, and yet the Challenger didn't get into the left lane to pass me, as numerous other cars did.

And now that we were heading east, with the sun at a different angle, I could see who was maybe following me: a white male was on the passenger side and a brown-skinned man was driving. And they looked large and wide. Too big for the front seat of the Challenger. So maybe they *were* detectives. Cops often come in large.

They were close on my tail, and I opened my window — it was getting pretty hazy in the car from my joint — and sent them an obscure smoke signal, written in cannabis, which didn't merit a response.

So there we were, my Caprice and their Challenger, meandering like a tandem — *if* we were a tandem — down Franklin, and my office was five minutes away on Vermont, but wanting to test something, I hung a quick right onto Garfield Place without putting on my signal.

Following so close, the Challenger seemed to take the turn a little late, but it still managed to make the right onto Garfield and have it look *somewhat* intentional.

Fifty yards later, I pulled over to the side of the road.

They drove on past, feigning disinterest, I imagined.

But because of their tinted windows, I couldn't get a look at the white man on the passenger side, which was frustrating, and maybe it was all a coincidence.

So I just sat there, smoking, and watched the muscle car make its way down Garfield — a street of squat apartment buildings — and the light in the sky was violet-hued and beautiful. The sun must have just dipped into the Pacific, cooling itself and turning Los Angeles, as it did each day, into a purple city.

Then the Challenger crossed Hollywood Boulevard, disappearing from my line of sight, and so I did a quick U-turn and headed back up to Franklin.

Five minutes later, I turned right on Vermont, went down two blocks, and then parked my car in the quiet, narrow alleyway behind the Dresden bar.

I put my joint in the ashtray, grabbed my thermos, and as I slammed my door, it didn't really surprise me to see the Challenger coming down the alley, glowering in its dark paint job.

I could have run or got back into my car, but there was the feeling that I would only be delaying the inevitable, and so I waited for them in the beautiful light. It was what they call in the movie business *magic hour*.

The Challenger parked right behind my Caprice, blocking it, and the two men boiled out, moving fast for their size. They were both about six four, 250, like brother slabs of beef in a meat market.

The white beef looked like a farm boy from the Midwest, and the brown beef looked Hawaiian. Midwest had blonde hair buzzed down like a peach and Hawaii had black hair pulled back tight in a ponytail.

They both were wearing jeans and sneakers and hoodies, and they had that look. A look that said they wanted to hurt someone. That someone being me.

I did a quick scan of the alley for witnesses, but we were all alone. On the plus side, these two didn't seem to be cops. Their eyes were too eager: violent but maybe not cruel.

So I put my thermos on the roof of my car, like it was a casual thing to do, and I fingered the steel baton I was carrying in my sport-jacket pocket, because I needed *something* to even the odds. There were 500 pounds of them and only 190 pounds of me, most of it alchemized silvery fish from a can.

"You boys seem to know where I live and where I work," I said, as they came to the front of the Challenger and were about six feet away. "How can I help you?"

I pegged them to be in their early thirties and I called them "boys" because I was fifty-one and missing a kidney, which made me more like sixty-one. When you lose an organ you lose a decade of your life, someone told me. Which is probably not true, but it's a good line when you're looking for sympathy.

"Yeah, you can help us," said Midwest. "You can help us remember Carl Lusk."

That's when I knew for certain the baton needed to make an appearance, and I brought it out and snapped it to its full sixteen-inch length. It's one of those extendable steel batons you can buy on the internet if you're a wannabe fascist or in the security business like me.

Midwest saw my weapon, but it didn't scare him — probably because he had never been hit by one — and he took two big steps forward, with his fist cocked, and as he threw his haymaker, I took a step to my right and slashed down on his wrist, breaking something, and he went straight to the ground, mewling.

Then Hawaii charged me, going for a tackle, and I squatted and swiped at his knees with the baton and heard a nice crunch, which made him come up short and fall, but he still was able to knock me to the asphalt, and I landed hard on my ass, with half of him on top of me.

I then hit him brutally across the back of his broad shoulders, which he definitely felt, and I was able to push him off me, like pushing off a piano, and Midwest was still on his knees, wailing; his hand was hanging from his wrist at a weird angle.

I stood up, a little slowly, panting from the adrenaline and the fear and hitting the ground hard, and Hawaii also stood up, quicker than I expected, and he punched me in the face, a nice shot to the left cheekbone, and I staggered back and faltered, which made him hopeful.

He then rushed me with a looping punch, and I jumped up — I don't know where the instinct came from — and I hit him on the top of his head with the baton, like chopping a piece of wood, and he went down face-first into the pavement.

He wasn't knocked out, but he didn't get up. He curled into a ball, grabbed the top of his head, and vomited. Then I looked around. My fight with these two had lasted less than a minute and the alleyway was still empty: no one had seen anything.

I didn't want to go near the vomit, and so I limped over to Midwest and he looked up at me like a child.

His pain had made him innocent again, but not too innocent, and I raised the baton up into the air, like I was going to strike him, but I was just bluffing, playing the tough guy, and I said, "Give me your phone."

He obediently reached into his hoodie pocket with his good hand and gave me the phone. I bypassed his code, hitting the word EMERGENCY in the lower-left corner, and put it on speaker.

"I called 911," I said. "Keep me out of it and I won't press charges. And I won't hit you again."

I handed him the phone — we could both hear it ringing through the speaker — and he just looked at me; he was in some kind of shock, holding his arm out away from his body, like it scared him, which I could understand.

His hand was dangling off his wrist like a dead bird, and I said, "I'm very sorry about Carl Lusk."

And I meant it.

Then a woman's neutral voice came out of the phone: "This is 911, what is your emergency?"

Midwest then put the phone in front of his mouth, looked at me, and mumbled, "I've been in an accident."

Satisfied, I grabbed my thermos off the Caprice and went quickly through the back door of the Dresden. There was time enough for a swift drink before my meeting, and I wanted some ice for my face.

2.

BILLY, MIDDLE-AGED, BALD, and slim-hipped from cocaine, was behind the bar and the place was empty. The Dresden had just opened. It was five p.m.: happy hour, no pun intended. I took my regular stool, and Billy, knowing what I drink and how I take it, came over with a bottle of Don Julio and poured me *half* a shot in a tumbler and added ice.

Marijuana, I abuse. Alcohol, I absorb like medicine. In small doses. Been like that for a while. Even when I had *two* kidneys.

I nodded at Billy, said, "Thanks," and I took a spinstery sip, and right away the tequila mixed nicely with whatever weed was left in my system. I was smoking so much then that the stuff died quick in me. At that point it was practically a placebo.

Billy watched me and said, "What happened to your face?"

"My beauty mark?" I said, half joking.

"No, your new one."

I looked in the bar mirror behind Billy and a nice marble-size lump was already forming on my left cheekbone, and the beauty mark I had referred to was just beneath the marble: a four-inch scar that goes straight down to my jawline like a zipper.

I touched the marble gently and said to Billy, "I opened up my engine all screwy and clipped myself with the hood. Could you put some ice in a napkin for me?"

Billy knew I wasn't telling the truth — bartenders are wonderful lie detectors — but he didn't challenge me on it. Dealing coke on the side had killed a lot of Billy's brain, but he had learned one important life lesson: *Keep your mouth shut more than you open it.*

"Sure, a little ice," he said, "no problem," and with a shrug at my lie, he grabbed a napkin and bent over the ice bin. The bar lights glinted off his bald skull, and I thought of Hawaii outside, holding the top of his head.

Billy passed me the ice and I pressed it against the marble.

"Seen Monica?" I asked, in a moment of weakness.

"Nah," he said. And then he left me there. Abruptly. Like I said, he was a closemouthed type, and then some other drinkers came in to keep Billy busy, and I took another sip of my tequila.

The Dresden doesn't have any windows — it's a dark, shadowy lounge with red-leather booths and a hardworking piano — and I was tempted to go back outside and see if the ambulance had arrived yet, to see if those boys were okay, but it was smarter to stay right where I was and *not* return to the scene of the crime.

So I swirled the tequila under my tongue, homeopathically, and then I lowered the ice from my face. I was hoping that somehow the swelling would already be going down before my meeting, but I looked in the bar mirror and it wasn't down, it was getting bigger, and I put the ice back on.

And my beauty mark — the ugly scar that *Carl Lusk* had given me — also looked like shit. It looked like a thin pink worm dying on a sidewalk after a rainstorm; the kind you pick up and put in the grass and hope for the best, but you know it won't make it.

Lusk, whom Midwest had wanted "help" remembering, was an ex–football player for USC, an All-American offensive lineman, and I figured those two boys outside had been his teammates, maybe fellow line mates, and I knew why they had come looking for me.

Nine months earlier, I had been working security at the Miracle Thai Spa, on Argyle and Franklin, and Carl Lusk came in one night and started smoking meth in the salt-scrub room. A girl named Mei was doing his scrub and the meth hit Carl funny. He tried to strangle Mei, tried to kill her, but she managed to scream, and then I entered the picture. With my baton.

Unfortunately, he had come to the spa with a big hunting knife — stashed in the backpack he had brought with him — and so then it became knife versus baton.

And knife won.

He cut my face in half.

Then I took my gun out.

Which wasn't really fair, and I was hoping to just slow him down, but there was blood in my eyes, and I shot him, unintentionally, in the neck, and he died at my feet.

It was nothing to be proud of, in fact it was the opposite, and he was the first man I had ever killed. But I wasn't charged. It was deemed self-defense, and Mei, thankfully, survived.

The local news and the papers ran with it for a second — EX-USC STAR KILLED AT SPA — but then it quickly faded away and the world seemed to forget about Carl Lusk.

But now, nine months later, Midwest and Hawaii had come out of the woodwork because Carl was back in the news. His father, Bill Lusk, a well-known and decorated homicide detective, had committed suicide on Christmas Day by jumping off the Vincent Thomas Bridge in the Los Angeles Harbor. A movie director had done it once and there have been a number of copycats since.

When Lusk jumped the whole gruesome thing was caught on somebody's phone, which he must have wanted, his grief to be broadcast far and wide on Christmas Day, and all the articles said he had killed himself because he couldn't get over what had happened to his son.

What especially hurt Lusk, according to one columnist in the *LA Times,* was that the man who killed his boy — me, the lowly security guard — was an ex-cop. A member of the LAPD brotherhood. Which made it even more of a betrayal for Lusk. He had given his life to the force and his son had been gunned down like a felon. Which he was. A felon. And that must have been one more thing Bill Lusk couldn't accept and so he took it to the bridge.

All this brought my name back into circulation, and so Carl's old teammates — I had to figure they were ex–football players, it was the only thing that would account for their size — had done some clever googling, found me, and I had hurt them. Which I regretted. I probably should have run away. In Buddhism, you're not to cause pain; the whole idea is to *lessen* the suffering of others, not increase it.

I finished my tequila and stood up. I left a ten on the bar, exited out the front, and then walked down Vermont to my office. The light was no longer purple. Magic hour was over.

3.

BY 5:15, I HAD the key in the door of my professional chambers, which are on the second floor of a two-story building, half a block from the Dresden. My office was originally a storeroom back in the day, and it's shaped like a coffin, long and narrow, and doesn't quite seem normal. It's more like a room in a dream: all distorted and elongated, where things happen that don't make sense.

But you can't beat the rent. It's frozen in place around 1979, when human beings could still afford things, which is a favor to me because I know the landlord and he's partial in my direction. Which is my fancy way of saying he likes me.

A while back, I helped him with his painful divorce — his brother was sleeping with his wife, a grotesque double betrayal — and I nursed him through a three-day suicidal breakdown after I gave him the news. Since then, he gives me the office for practically nothing as a kind of lifelong thank-you, though I'm not sure anybody else would rent it.

But that doesn't matter. I need a place to meet clients that's private and a little obscure to give them a sense of comfort and anonymity, and if the office exudes a dingy feeling that's okay. It matches what they're coming to see me for, and so in an odd way it puts them at ease. They think: *Here's someone who will get dirty for me.*

To give it a little class, though, some pictures of me in the Navy and the

LAPD hang on the wall, and there's a show filing cabinet with nothing in it, and a printer that makes half decent photos if I get divorce work, which isn't too often.

When I let myself in that day, the office was nearly pitch-black, but I didn't turn on the ceiling light. I wanted to be able to look out the window without any glare.

I pulled up the blinds and down below was the alleyway. Night was coming on fast, and I pressed my face against the cool window to help with the swelling, and my timing was perfect. Just then an ambulance, with flashing lights, drove past — on its way out — and I felt relieved. The football players would be taken care of, and I had ten minutes to further gather myself before my appointment. Which was with a woman named Mary DeAngelo, who had contacted me through my rather simple website the day before, writing that she needed help locating her mother and did I do that kind of work? I said I did, and we set the meeting.

She didn't ask me about my fee in her emails and I didn't bring it up, not wanting to scare her off. I always ask for four hundred a day, but I'm a weak negotiator and I'll slide all the way down to a hundred a day, especially if it's in cash.

And truth is, I've been known to go as low as fifty a day. You can buy a lot of sardines with fifty bucks, and I'm not proud. *Or* successful. But I work for myself and that's something.

My website indicates that I'm a "security specialist," which is a vague term that covers a lot of ground. I used to be a licensed private investigator — had a license for over fifteen years — but I lost it shortly after Carl Lusk opened my face and I killed him in self-defense.

But that's not why I lost it.

Later in the same week that I killed Carl Lusk, I uncovered a doctor in Malibu who specialized in performing very expensive black-market organ transplants.

The doctor's patients, whom he treated at his compound in the Malibu hills, were very wealthy people who didn't want to wait on line — or couldn't survive waiting on line — in the straight world, and so they came to the black market for the organs they needed and would pay whatever was asked. It was a lucrative business.

I stumbled into the whole thing trying to help a friend, and in uncovering the doctor, who had killed twenty-three migrants in order to harvest their bodies, I broke a number of laws and had my license taken away.

I also lost my kidney. The doctor, a man named Madvig, took it out of me and put it in one of his patients. Later, I killed Madvig and two of the men he worked with.

Not out of revenge, really, but to escape from being further stripped.

This all happened back in March of 2019, and just a few days after the Carl Lusk story, I got even more coverage in the *LA Times:* PRIVATE INVESTIGATOR UNCOVERS GRUESOME SCENE IN MALIBU: TWENTY-THREE BODIES FOUND.

And after the story broke, I suddenly had a lot of business but also no license.

So I quickly reinvented myself as a "security specialist" and was doing the same things I had done before to help people, but with less protection under the law.

But I didn't care. I was happy for the work.

Before that I had been broke for a long time and had been scraping by as a glorified bouncer at the Miracle spa, but now, just nine months later, things had already dried up again, which is why I was hoping that Mary DeAngelo would have money to spend — even fifty a day — and that she would hire me. I had a little less than a thousand in the bank, and I didn't want to go back to working at the spa. It hadn't been so good for my health the last time.

And just then, on cue, there was a timid knock at my door, and I turned away from the window. Turned away from the sight of the ambulance carrying off the vanquished football players.

But I did a quick bit of tonglen for them. That's this Buddhist thing, like a prayer, where you breathe in someone's pain — all their confusion and heartbreak and sorrow — and then when you breathe out, you send them well-being and love, like you're an antenna of some kind.

And they don't know you've done this.

But maybe they do.

And then there was another timid knock at my door.

Mary DeAngelo was a few minutes early, and right then would have been a good time to get one of those telegrams from the back of my brain that alerted me to danger. But no messages were sent. Or maybe I wasn't home to receive them, and I said, "Come in."

4.

I TURNED ON THE desk lamp, which gave the room a nice glow, and the door opened slowly. Then she teetered in — a little wobbly — on large, blocky heels, and gave me a shy smile.

Tall and willowy, strange and beautiful, she came through that door like someone coming in from another time. In her right hand was a small vintage purse, maybe big enough for a wallet or a small gun.

"Ms. DeAngelo?"

"Yes," she said, and then she looked away. The pink worm on my face often caused that reaction.

"Come in, come in," I said cheerily.

She closed the door behind her. "I'm sorry I'm early."

"Not a problem," I said, and she wobbled on those big heels toward me. She was wearing a black cotton dress with some kind of lacy frill at the top — it had a vintage-shop look — and draped around her shoulders was an old brown men's cardigan, overly big.

She was young, somewhere in her early twenties, and her hair was cut short, with a bang of sleek black curls arranged on her forehead like a line of musical notes, and I noticed as she got closer that her left eye, an eerie pale green, was off-center and seemed to be staring at the photos on the wall.

And the right eye, equally pale green and equally eerie, bore down on me, cyclopically.

The off-kilter eye flawed her beauty, making it even greater, and she had an elegant long nose and a full mouth, painted a violent red, and there were no wrinkles in her bluish-white, almost translucent skin.

She looked like a flapper, and I stepped around my desk and offered my hand. Her cold hand went in mine, and her long fingernails were painted carmine or dipped in blood, and the bones of her fingers felt like the spines of bird feathers.

"So nice to meet you," I said, and I could smell her perfume, sandalwood, and I flashed, painfully, for a moment, to a woman I had loved, and there was a fragmentary vision — of the beloved rushing out of a shop to greet me — and then I returned to the present.

"Nice to meet *you*," the young woman said, looking at me with her one eye, and the effect was compelling. It made the way she looked at you more intense, more intimate than maybe it was.

Then I released her hand. "Please, sit down," I said, and I pulled on the back of the client chair, making a little space for her, like a waiter in a French movie, or a French restaurant, for that matter.

She sat down, and then I sat down across from her. Between us was my old gray metal desk, which in its youth worked for the post office on North Alvarado. I had bought it at auction for five dollars, and I could sometimes feel the ghosts of the postal workers who had sat behind it for decades, their lives ticking by like all lives, clocks meant to run down.

On top of the desk were three items of interest: a stone paperweight with a painting of my dog, George, on it; a coffee mug with a photograph of my dog, George, on it; and a 1950s sculpted coffee mug of Lou Costello's face, which I use for pens and other office detritus.

"Traffic all right?" I said, to kick things off.

"Fine," she said.

"Where were you coming from?"

"West Hollywood."

"Oh, I'm glad it wasn't too bad."

"I took an Uber. Just looked out the window," she said.

Then she gave me a sad, melancholic smile, a life weariness came over her, and that exhausted the preliminaries and we lapsed into silence.

To fill the gap, I took a pad out of my top drawer, a blue spiral notebook that I had bought at the supermarket in the school-supply section. I'm old-fashioned in that I like to write things down, which also means that a fair amount of doodling takes place. Then I took a pen out of Lou Costello's head and scrawled at the top of the page, *Mary DeAngelo,* and the date, *1/10/20.*

That was a very symmetrical date and I noticed that my hand was sort of trembling, but I ignored it. I said, "You don't mind if I take notes, do you?"

"No," she said.

Then I realized I had forgotten my manners and said, "I'm so sorry. I should have asked. Would you like a cup of coffee?" I indicated my thermos and the mug with the photograph of George.

"No, thank you," she said. She was a very polite young woman, and she spoke like she looked: formal and a little whispery, circa 1926.

"The mug is clean if that's an issue," I said. "It's for clients."

"I don't drink coffee in the afternoon," she said. "If I do, my nerves get all jangly, like a swarm of bees."

I enjoyed her imagery — it was florid and peculiar and hinted, perhaps, at a disturbed intelligence — and I said, "That's sensible. Do you mind if I have a cup?"

"Not at all," she said, and I smiled at her in gratitude, unscrewed the top of the thermos, which acts like a cup, and poured myself a bit of the restorative.

While I did this, she waved her hand at the George mug and the George stone and said, "Who's that?"

I turned the mug with the George photo toward her so she could get the full effect of his liquid eyes. "That's my dog, George," I said. "We're very close."

"He's beautiful," she said.

"I won't disagree with you," I said.

In the picture, George, who is half Chihuahua, half terrier, is looking over his shoulder at me. With a lot of feeling.

"He has dreamy eyes like the *Girl with a Pearl Earring* by Vermeer," she said, sounding quite Ivy League and affected. The cadence of her speech was sophisticated, practiced, and made her sound older than she was.

"That's a painting?"

"Oh, yes," she said. "Very famous. For the eyes. For beautiful eyes."

"I'll look it up," I said and smiled at her crookedly; a few nerves in my face had died when Carl Lusk cut me. Then I lifted my thermos cup to have a sip and my hand was really shaking. I wondered what the hell was going on — was it the sandalwood? — and then suddenly I knew what it was. The fight in the alleyway had impacted me more than I realized, and I put the cup down.

"Are you all right?" she asked. "You have a…bruise."

She didn't want me to think she was referring to my scar — *or* my trembling hands — and she pointed, with a long finger, as white as a piano key, at the swelling on my cheekbone, and it was then that I noticed the oversize diamond wedding ring on her left hand. She seemed too young to be married, let alone with a stone on her finger that was smaller than a hard-boiled egg but not by a lot.

"I'm fine," I said, touching my swollen cheekbone. "I have an old car and when I checked the oil, the hood caught me on the way up."

"Oh," she said, and she probably believed me as much as Billy had back in the bar, which meant I was off my game. Usually I'm quite good at lying — I have a knack for it after a lifetime of self-deception — and so I needed to rally and get things on track with this young woman. With a diamond ring that size, she might be able to pay me my full fee. I said, "Tell me what's going on. How can I help you? You mentioned that you wanted to find your mother."

"Yes…"

"What's the situation? Why does she need to be found?"

"The situation is —"

Then she looked down and went silent. I managed then to take a sip of my coffee, without spilling any, to give *her* time and to help *me* get a grip on myself, to move on from the fight and shove it back down with all the other fights.

Then she looked back up and said, "The situation is that my mother is homeless, and I haven't heard from her in two months and I'm worried."

"How long has she been homeless?"

"I think five or six years. She's a junkie. Plus mental illness. Hard to say what. Not quite schizophrenia, but she's not of this world, really."

"I'm sorry," I said, putting the right amount of gravity into my voice, and she nodded, accepting my sympathies, and then I added, "Do you know where she stays? Her haunts? Skid Row? Venice?"

"No. She's not in Los Angeles. She's homeless up in Olympia. Washington. I haven't seen her for thirteen years, not since I was eleven, when she left LA." That made her twenty-four; the blue-sponge sport jacket I was wearing was about the same age. "But then a few months ago she found me on Facebook and we started talking on the phone. She uses the kind of phone you get at Target or something, you buy minutes, but it's not in service anymore and we haven't spoken since November, and I'm worried because it's winter up there. She's sixty years old."

"Have you tried messaging her on Facebook?"

"No. We only used it that one time. She said she joined it to find me. She didn't have any friends or pictures or anything. And I deleted my account a few months ago. Didn't want to be on there anymore."

"Have you contacted the Olympia police?"

"No. I don't think the police would do much. And not with any urgency."

"You're probably right. Have you made any calls to hospitals or shelters?" I left out *morgues*.

"A few, but then I got overwhelmed, and no one would tell me anything anyway. That's why I need a professional."

"Right. So what about someone in my field in Olympia? Or a big city nearby, like Seattle? Have you looked into that?"

"No. You're the first person I've contacted."

There's no money in this for me, I thought, and I said, "Well, you're better off with someone who knows Olympia. I can ask around. Get some names for you."

"No. I want to hire *you.* It's kismet."

I didn't like the sound of that. I'm into Buddhism but not mystical mumbo jumbo, which is usually a product of deluded wishful thinking. Regardless, I kept a poker face and said, "Why's it kismet?"

"Because I saw your name in the paper. About the policeman. And I never read the paper, but I did the other day and so that was the first sign." She leaned forward then, put her hands on my desk. "And the second thing is that my mother told me about you a long time ago. Said there was a man named Happy Doll who was a sad doll and called himself Hank. And I never forgot it. She also told me that if I ever needed help that I should come to you. So here I am. I need help."

The intensity of her feeling centered, momentarily, her lazy eye, and I got a cold feeling down my neck. That article in the newspaper was bringing me all sorts of bad karma, and like all karma it was of my own making. I said, "I know your mother?"

"Yes. I'm sorry I didn't tell you right away. I thought you might not want to see me. I know she burned a lot of bridges back in the day and that she was your girlfriend for a little while. My mother is Ines Candle."

This I wasn't expecting at all, and her name hung in the air between us, like the way Ines was the last time I had seen her: she was naked in her tub and both her arms were slit, like envelopes, from wrist to elbow, and they were just floating out in front of her in the blood-pink water.

But she wasn't dead.

I had got there in time, and when I lifted her out of the tub, bloody and wet like a newborn, her eyes opened and she gave me that charming, rueful smile of hers. The one that seemed to say, "Can you believe this mess?"

A few days after that, arms sewed up like a ripped pair of jeans, she left LA, and I never heard from her again. The first few years, I sometimes thought of trying to find her, but I didn't do anything about it because I knew she didn't want to be found. She had left that way out of kindness, to save me from myself.

But now she was back. In the form of her daughter.

5.

I LOOKED AT THE GIRL and tried to maintain my poker face, but if there was a tell it would have been the despair in my eyes. I wasn't shocked to hear that Ines was homeless, but, still, I was saddened by it. I said, finally, "It's been a long time since I've seen your mother. You know, you wear the same scent. Sandalwood."

Maybe I *did* believe in mumbo jumbo.

Or at least in the profound connection between smell and memory: it was Ines I had flashed to so vividly when I shook the girl's hand.

But even though Mary had the same dark hair and the same pale green eyes as Ines, they looked nothing alike, and I never would have guessed that this was Ines's child. A child I had never met, until now. And I remembered Ines referring to her daughter, Mary, but I never knew the girl's last name. When I got that email from Mary DeAngelo it never occurred to me that I would be meeting Ines's daughter, *her* Mary.

"I didn't know that about the sandalwood," she said. "But maybe that's why I wear it. It reminds me of her, and I didn't realize it...When did you see my mother last?"

"I also haven't seen her for thirteen years."

"That makes sense. It was thirteen years ago that she tried to kill herself. Then after that, she disappeared." She looked down at her hands and a sadness passed over her and seemed to fill my office with its feeling, its weather, and then she looked back up at me. "And I don't want to lose her again. Which is why I'm here."

I knew where this was going, but this wasn't a job I wanted to take, and so I said to her, stalling, "You have a good memory to recall that business about my name." What I didn't tell her was that a few months after I lost my kidney, I stopped calling myself Hank, like a bald man letting go of his toupee, and had finally accepted the name my parents had saddled me with: *Happy. Happy Doll.* They hadn't meant for it to be a joke.

"I do have a good memory," she said. "I'm cursed with remembering everything. So will you help me, Mr. Doll? She's the only family I have left."

"What about your father?"

"He and my stepmother died in a car accident when I was fifteen. She was driving *and* she was drunk. My father loved addicts. It's what killed him."

"I'm sorry," I said. Her life made for a lot of apologies. "Who took care of you after they passed?"

"Nobody. I was in foster care briefly but then I ran away and was on my own for a long time. So, you see, I know what it's like to be homeless and why my mother is in danger."

Then her lips snarled, unconsciously, at something remembered, and her face hardened, and she wasn't a flapper anymore. I saw street on her, and I knew that look on her face.

When I was a cop, I worked juvenile in the Hollywood Division, which meant runaways and sex trafficking and homelessness, and I had met a lot of girls with a story like Mary's, a story that invariably included the horror of assault and living with the constant hideous threat of more assault, and so what I saw on her face I'd seen many times before. It said, "I trust no one. And come too close and I'll kill you."

I wanted to say I was sorry again — for the *third* time — but it had rung a little hollow the first time. "So will you help me?" she said, filling in the silence, and her features softened back into the mannered, demure mask she had walked in with. "Will you help me find my mother?"

I wasn't sure what to say, though I could hear my psychoanalyst's voice dimly in my head: "Don't do it. Don't get involved. Take care of yourself."

To avoid the girl's singular eye, I swiveled in my chair a little and glanced out the window, pretending that something had occurred to me. It was already pitch-black outside, and I was caught off guard by my own reflection. The window was a darkened mirror, and my face, lit by the desk lamp, looked like the ghoulish face of a dead man you might see floating by in a river, just below the surface. For a moment, I thought, spooked, *Who's out there?*

Then I realized it was me, and I turned back to Mary and told her I would take the job, because how could I say no to her? This was the daughter of Ines Candle. Her birthright was tragedy. *Somebody* had to help her.

6.

"YOU'LL REALLY DO IT?"

"Yes. I can start here in LA, making some calls. And if that doesn't turn her up, I'll go to Olympia."

She was expressionless, deadpan, and then suddenly she started to cry, and her face shattered, like a building detonated from the inside, and she leaned forward, hiding her face in her hands. "Sorry," she said, teary-voiced. "This is a great relief."

The emotion seemed real enough, but the way she cried was like out of a movie, a silent movie: overwrought and very damsel-in-distress. "I'll get you a tissue," I said, standing up, awkward and helpless.

I left the office and went down the hall to the men's room. I grabbed her some toilet paper, and by the time I got back she had pulled herself together and was putting her phone back into her purse.

I handed her the toilet paper anyway. "Sorry, it's not Kleenex."

"Thank you," she said, and dabbed at her eyes with the coarse paper.

Then as discreetly and as femininely as possible, she somehow blew her nose without any sound. I sat back down and said, "Naturally, I won't charge you my full fee —"

"That's ridiculous," she said, cutting me off angrily. "I'm married to a wealthy man. I'm not a street urchin anymore, *Mr. Doll*."

She seemed irrationally and disproportionately offended, and it was increasingly hard to get a bead on her, but then I thought, *Ines's daughter*, like that explained it all, and maybe it did.

"I'm sorry," I said. "I didn't mean anything by it. Just that I knew your mother and we were close once. Anyway, my full fee is four hundred a day—"

"That's fine," she said, cutting me off. "Money is not an issue, but my husband would like to meet you tomorrow night at the Tower Bar at eight. We texted while you were in the bathroom. Do you know the Tower?" One-eyed and Janus-faced, she kept changing in front of me like a flip-book: a flapper, a street girl, a crying maiden, and now a curt and officious lady in charge.

"I know the Tower," I said. "Your husband wants to look me over?" I meant it as a joke, but it came out defensive.

"Yes. But it's a formality," she said, softening again. "He knows this is important to me and he'll give you a check then. And if whatever calls you are going to make don't scare up my mother, do you think you can leave for Olympia on Sunday? I know it's short notice, but is it possible?"

"I can make Sunday work. But let's see first if she's somewhere in the system."

"Good. My husband's assistant will be the one to help arrange your travel. *If* you have to fly north." She then reached into her purse and drew out five one-hundred-dollar bills and put them on my desk, slightly fanned out so I could see the amount. "Here's a retainer. To get you started."

I looked at the crisp bills. She had laid them out like a john putting money down on a bedside table. "Looks like you knew I'd say yes."

"Not exactly. I was *hoping* you'd say yes."

"And if I do find her, then what?"

"We'll get her off the streets. Put her in a hotel or something, and then my husband and I will arrange for some kind of housing. I wasn't ready before…the drugs…but even if she's a junkie I want her safe."

"I understand."

She nodded and then suddenly got out of her chair, ending our meeting, once more the officious lady in charge, and said, "Well, we'll see you tomorrow night, Mr. Doll. The reservation will be under my husband's name. Marrow. Hoyt Marrow."

"Marrow like bone marrow?"

"Yes," she said, and started to leave then, and I caught up to her and opened my office door for her, like a gentleman, and being so close, I could smell the sandalwood again. But also something else: something sharp and uric. Something sick. It hadn't been there before.

I said, "A quick question before you go. Do you have any pictures of your mother?"

"No. She didn't send me any pictures from her phone. I got the feeling, of course, that she was in rough shape. It's sad but I've just about forgotten what she looks like."

"Anything from your childhood? From thirteen years ago?"

"Nothing," she said. "Everything from my childhood was lost when my father died. Do *you* have any pictures of her?"

"I don't think so. I've never taken a lot of photos."

"See, this is why it's kismet. If she's not in a hospital or a shelter, no one else could find her. Except you. You know what she looks like."

Then she offered me her chilly hand. I took it, and she said, "We'll see you tomorrow night." Then she bowed her head in goodbye and stepped out into the hallway. I stood in the open door and watched her wobble off down the hall to the staircase, clutching her sweater to her throat.

I held my hand up in a salute of farewell, and I waited, but she didn't look back.

I retreated then to my desk and got a joint out of the top drawer.

I smoked and nervously doodled.

I did a bunch of shaded-in triangles, and then I did a drawing of a tormented man, and there was nothing new about him. I've been drawing variations of this fellow for decades, and oftentimes, though not always, he looks like a version of me, just more distorted, with bug eyes and a crooked, phallic nose.

Then I quit the artwork and looked at myself in the darkened window. The girl had rattled me — what was that sickly smell? Fear? Disease? And I wondered if I should back out. It would be easy enough. It's what my analyst, Dr. Lavich, would want me to do.

But then I felt it. The hook in my mouth. Why I really had said yes.

I wanted to see Ines again.

7.

I WALKED OVER TO the Drawing Room, a dive bar a few blocks away on Hillhurst Avenue. It's in a little strip mall, right next to a laundromat, and it's a nasty, dark place with a semicircle bar and old leather stools.

There are also a few cracked-leather booths, a pool table, a jukebox, and a disgusting bathroom where people key shit cocaine — cut with foot powder — into their nose. Or at least they used to. And I know because I was in there doing it. But that was a long time ago.

The bar wasn't too busy yet — the Friday night crowd was just starting to get its drink on — and the bartender, who had ginger-colored rockabilly sideburns he was proud of and a belly like a tumor, came over to me, and I ordered another shot of tequila, in honor of Ines. It was in the Drawing Room that I had met her.

And as I sipped my drink, I closed my eyes and time traveled. It's something I like to do more and more as I get older. I don't have a lot of pictures documenting my life, but I have memories, and what I do is sensuously and vividly recall some location, some place in time, and I'm there again, and it feels real. Or close to real.

Usually, I'm not in the exact spot, like right then at the bar. Mostly I'm in bed while I zip around in my life, a waking dream state where I visit with old girlfriends, or I'm in Seoul on leave, or I go back to childhood, to

San Diego, and I'm ten years old and having dinner with my dad, who hated my guts but now I miss him.

This time, though, I was right in the Drawing Room, with my eyes closed, and it was the Drawing Room I went back to and what I saw on the screen in my mind was Ines sitting at the end of the bar again, like that first night, and she looks up at me from her drink and smiles.

She's wearing a man's white oxford shirt, several buttons open offering a shadowy glimpse inside, and her long black hair, streaked with iron gray, is pulled back tight from her forehead and goes down her neck, like a thick rope.

Her skin is olive-sallow and without wrinkles, and her face is fierce, handsome. The skin is tight around the forehead, the bones are pronounced, and her cheekbones are also severe and defined, partly because her cheeks are a little sunken, some kind of privation and suffering there, drawing down to a gentle, well-shaped mouth, with lips more purple than red.

Her nose, at the end, curves down slightly, almost hawkishly, and she wears no makeup, and her beautiful green eyes are curious, unafraid, and maybe a little mad.

Then, still smiling, she swivels in her stool to face me directly, she's wearing jeans and ankle boots, and she's not tall and willowy like her daughter, she's compact and coiled, built like a gymnast, and she pats the open stool next to her, indicating that I should join her. "Buy a lady a drink?" she asks. I sit next to her and buy her a drink.

Then I opened my eyes and did the math.

She would have been forty-seven then and I was thirty-eight.

Then I closed my eyes again and time traveled to her old loft building downtown on Hooper Avenue, near Skid Row. It's a few weeks after meeting her at the bar, and she has a roommate and when money gets tight, she rents out her small bedroom in the apartment and lives on the roof in a tent, using the bathroom and the kitchen down below when she needs to.

The landlord, who is never around, doesn't know this, and so I climb the metal ladder that goes up the wall on the top floor and then I open the hatch in the roof, and there's Ines sitting in a beach chair, next to her tent, getting ready for being homeless way back then, and she's smoking a cigarette and drinking sake, and she pours me a drink, and I sit in the other beach chair she has up there, and we watch the sunset from the best spot downtown. Then after, with the sky a dark purple like a plum, we go into the tent, and she reaches for me —

A voice said, harshly, "No nodding out at the bar."

I opened my eyes. It was the ginger-haired bartender with the tumor-belly. I was back in January 2020, back in the present, back at the Drawing Room, and I didn't want to be there, and I forgot my Buddhism and said, "Fuck you, asshole," adding yet again, mindlessly, more violence to the world, more bad karma.

"No, fuck *you,* scar-face. Pay up and get out of here."

Some of the other patrons looked at us, expectant, feeling the electricity of anger, and the bartender's hand was reaching under the bar, maybe for a baseball bat, and I thought of sending my fist into his distended belly, but he was in the right, and I stood up and placed on the bar one of the hundreds Mary had bought me with.

Then I walked away.

By the door, the bartender caught my eye and gave me the finger, but then a big smile blossomed on his ugly face, like an open wound between his orange sideburns, and he said, waving the hundred, "Come back anytime."

8.

I STOPPED AT THE Gelson's market on Franklin and picked up a grass-fed New York strip for seventeen bucks and change. Even having tossed the bartender a hundred to clean up my karma, I was feeling flush, and I hadn't had meat in a while. Not since the money got tight.

In addition to the steak, I picked up a baguette, and from Gelson's I returned home to Glen Alder Street and parked in my stand-alone street-level garage. My house, which is on the hill above the garage, is an old, crumbling Spanish bungalow that was willed to me years ago by an elderly client after she passed.

To get to the house from the street, you have to climb twelve stairs, then pass through a wooden gate and fence and climb thirty-three more stairs, the equivalent, overall, of about two stories. My front yard, which the stairs run alongside, is an overgrown slope of wildflowers and weeds and bougainvillea, as well as several trees, which shroud the house in privacy.

And that night, as I climbed the dark stairs, through my little patch of forest, I felt very French. My baguette was in my hand, like a sword, and when I came through the front door, George jumped on me frantically, beside himself with joy, and I swatted him lovingly on his meager buttocks with the bread, like I was a fencing master, and said, "Down, young man," and then he attacked one of his toys, pretending to kill it as a way to work through his good feelings.

While he did this, I unwrapped the steak and left it out on the kitchen counter to get it to room temperature.

Then I took George for a walk, and back down the stairs we went.

When we hit the street, I delighted, as I often do, in the way he trotted along on his thin white legs. There's an inherent optimism to his canter and a strength of spirit that I very much admire, which I can't quite pull off myself, but at least I can see it in him.

After a block of quick trotting, he then began his usual dedicated hunt for the urine markings of fellow dogs, which he then covered over with his mark, and, of course, a lot of times when he lifted his leg nothing visible to the human eye came out, but I always imagine, in these instances, that some hormonal spray-signature is released, and I try my best never to rush him when he's smelling urine and marking as I know it's all very important to him, his life's work more or less, and so I use the time to study him, like a lover: his torso is golden-tan and sleek; his neck is white, like the collar of a formal shirt, and his head is brown with ears as soft as French velvet. And his eyes, as Mary DeAngelo had pointed out, are his most distinctive feature: large and amber-colored, full of love and sadness, like all the great poets, and they're rimmed with black as if by a mascara's wand.

He's certainly a perfectly proportioned little fellow, and in the ring, with his trunks off, he comes in at twenty-four pounds. His one flaw is what the dog professionals call "leash aggression," which means he goes nuts every time we see another dog, no matter their size. Supposedly this is because of his youth on the streets — he's a rescue, five or six years old — and when I walk him, we do a lot of zigzagging about, avoiding other dogs, but in stark contrast to his leash aggression, with humans he's pure love, to the point of being indiscriminate. He's liable to cozy up to most anybody, which does wound me sometimes, but I also like to see him make others happy.

That night it was rather cool and pleasant out — winter in Los Angeles is my favorite time of year — and we didn't encounter many other dogs, which was relaxing.

All in all, we walked for about thirty minutes, one of our usual loops around our neighborhood, Beachwood Canyon, which lies beneath the Hollywood sign, that beacon of saccharine dreams and gunplay opera, and on the way back up the stairs to the house, I used my small Maglite to light the way and scare off any skunks, since one time George and I were sprayed, an unfortunate incident in our history.

When we were safely inside, I oiled and then salted the New York strip, and let George lick the green Styrofoam packaging the steak had come in, which he went at ravenously.

On my ancient fry pan, I then cooked the strip precisely for four minutes on one side, then three on the other. The smoke alarm went off, as it always does, and George, disturbed by the noise, hid under the table where I take my meals, which is in the small living room off the kitchen.

When it was done, I put the steak on a plate by the kitchen sink and topped it with a healthy slice of butter.

Then I put it under some foil to let it rest for a few minutes and went upstairs to get my reading glasses and the novel I was involved with at the moment, which was *Watership Down,* a beautiful parable about a brave clan of rabbits in the English countryside. I was in a phase of revisiting the books of my youth — I had finished *Tarzan* a few nights before — and I've been a voracious reader all my life. In the Navy, because I always carried a book around, they called me "the Dictionary."

I especially love to read and eat, and when I came back downstairs, I put a pickle on my plate next to my steak, since I didn't have any other vegetables. Then I ripped off a piece of baguette, grabbed some horseradish sauce, and repaired to the living room for my feast.

I ate methodically and mindfully, thanking the grass-fed cow for helping me, and in between measured bites of pickle, bread, and steak, I enjoyed my novel.

When I finished eating, I put the plate down on the floor for George, as there were plenty of juices for him to lick, and I had also left for him about one-fifth of the steak as a tithing to the animal gods and because I do love that little dog.

As is his wont, George ate quickly, and I often wish he would eat more slowly, relish the flavors the way he relishes the smell of fellow dog urine, but I have to remind myself, it's in his DNA to rush: his ancestors had to fight over scraps; it was eat fast or die.

So, when we were done, sated like two lions after our New York strip, we went upstairs: George to our bed, and me to my small home office because I wanted to see what the computer might tell me about my old love Ines Candle, her daughter, Mary DeAngelo, and Mary's supposedly wealthy husband, Hoyt Marrow.

9.

I HAD STARTED SUBSCRIBING to a database popular with private investigators, and that and some exhaustive googling didn't turn up much on those three. They were elusive in a way that isn't so common these days — there was little to no trace of them.

First off, Hoyt Marrow was probably a phony name, or he was someone in the tech business and was able to have himself scrubbed, though this seemed unlikely. I did manage to come across two Hoyt Marrows, neither of whom I thought would be married to Mary DeAngelo: one was an eighty-six-year-old pastor in Missouri and the other was a dead man in Kentucky who had run a summer stock theater and died a bachelor.

Mary was almost equally invisible: no social media, which she had mentioned but was odd for someone her age; no financial records; no rental records; no property ownership; and no arrests. The only thing that came up was her father and stepmother's dual obituary, nine years before, which said at the end, "They are survived by their daughter, Mary."

Searching Ines was a little more fruitful, but not much: I got her birthday, August 10, 1959, and that she had a felony arrest six months before, but what it was for was unclear, even on my paid-for search engine. I assumed it was drugs.

There were also no pictures of Ines on the web, as Mary had said, and I was certain I didn't have any, because I might have looked at them over the years, and, regardless, a more recent photo and a more helpful one would be her mug shot, which a friend of mine in the Culver City PD could get for me. But I'd make that call the next day, not wanting to bother my friend on a Friday night.

Some further internet searching—not my forte, but I soldiered on the best I could—revealed that Ines's father had died in 2010, and his obituary indicated that he had been survived by his wife, Anna, and predeceased by his two sons, Ines's younger brothers.

There were no obituaries for her brothers, just small death notices, and the causes of death for her brothers were unclear, but I suspected severe alcoholism.

For Ines's mother there was a very recent death notice from a Seattle funeral parlor: she had died in a nursing home on Christmas Day, the same day that Bill Lusk had jumped off the bridge. Seeing Ines's mother's death notice, I wondered if Mary knew her grandmother had died and not said anything about it. But maybe she didn't know—Ines had run away and been cut off from her family long before Mary was born.

Ines had told me that her father, a brutal patriarch and heavy drinker, had beaten all three of his children and his wife, and with Ines there had also been sexual abuse; drunk, he'd crawl into bed with her, starting when she was thirteen. The mother, complicit in her weakness, did nothing to stop her husband—she was too brutalized herself to protect her children, especially her daughter.

So, Ines, when she was seventeen, in order to get away from her father, left the faith she had been raised in—an obscure and rigid Christian sect, an offshoot of the Jehovahs. Her family then shunned her, which was the custom of that group, and when I knew Ines, she had not spoken to any of them in decades, and this was reflected in her father's obituary and the death notices of her mother and brothers: Ines was not mentioned; the shunning had held true.

And what had also held true, I imagined, was Ines being cut off from her father's business, Candle Warehouses, which was based in her hometown of

Bellingham, a port city in northern Washington State. The family name was originally Candalaria—Ines was a mix of Spanish and Portuguese and Lummi, a tribe whose stolen land is part of Washington—but Candalaria had been Anglicized, a few generations back, for business purposes.

She had told me that her father's warehouses were successful and that her family had been well-off, despite her father's sociopathy *or* because of it, and the last thing the internet disclosed to me was that the company had been sold by her mother in 2014 for quite a lot of money, and I wondered where that windfall would be headed now that the mother had passed. The business had sold for nearly twenty-five million dollars, mostly for its real estate value on the Bellingham Bay waterfront, which had also been the conduit for Ines's initial escape from her family.

At seventeen, when she left their church, she became the mistress of a captain of a long-haul fishing boat, and he gave her a job as a cook on the boat. It was easier for the captain, a middle-aged man, to hide his young lover from his wife at sea, and what followed over the next thirty years for Ines, most of which I believed when she told me about it — and she liked to tell the story of her life — was the definition of picaresque. And tragic.

Around 1978, she was able, she told me, to get away from the captain, who was just another wretched version of her father, and her late teens and early twenties were spent working in the galleys on other boats—an unusual job for a young woman, but she pulled it off—and she was based mostly out of Sitka, Alaska.

Then she literally joined a small circus that was passing through Sitka and got trained as an acrobat. The circus meandered all year long, going as far north as Sitka in the summer and as far south as La Paz on the Sea of Cortez in the winter. She was with the circus for five years, which was owned and run by Mexicans, and that's what changed the way she spoke: her English became slightly accented with a singsong Spanish quality.

When she was twenty-seven, she met a handsome Mexican American drug dealer in La Paz, whom she said looked like the boxer Oscar De La Hoya. This De La Hoya look-alike then got her hooked on snorting cocaine and heroin, the two deadly snows — cocaine to get you going and heroin to bring you down — and she quit the circus and moved with him, in the mid-'80s, to Los Angeles.

She then spent the next year living the high life as his moll in the Hollywood Hills, until he was murdered by a bad cop who was on his payroll. She was hidden in the house and watched the cop shoot her boyfriend right by their pool, which he fell into and filled with his blood, just like Gatsby. When the cop left, she packed her bags and got out of there. She knew from the beginning it wouldn't last.

After that, for the next seven years, to survive, she worked the strip clubs in Hollywood — she was great on the pole because of being an acrobat, she said — and was able to pay for her drug habit and a small apartment in Thai Town.

It was in one of the strip clubs, the Seventh Veil, that she met the man who would become Mary DeAngelo's father — though Ines never told me his last name, just referred to him as "my ex, Jimmy-the-chef."

When she met him, Jimmy was a line cook at the Sunset Marquis Hotel and sober in AA. He became a regular at the Veil, tipping her good money for lap dances several nights a week, and after a few months of this, Ines said, they actually fell in love.

So she moved in with him, quit stripping, quit drugs, and started going with him to AA and NA meetings. He also helped get her a job as a prep cook at the Marquis, and she was good at it from all her years cooking on boats.

Then, after they were together a year, she gave birth, at age thirty-six, to Mary, and she and Jimmy got married. But when Mary was one, Ines had a bad relapse and couldn't get clean.

By the time the girl was two, Ines was shooting heroin in her foot, which made her not quite a junkie in her eyes, and Jimmy divorced her. She didn't get alimony or any kind of visitation rights, though DeAngelo, who was quickly remarried, let her see the girl every few months for an afternoon.

Ines loathed this setup, but there wasn't much she could do, except get sober, which she would try to do by going back to meetings, but she kept relapsing, until she finally gave up trying altogether: the pull of the drugs and the pull of her past were too great, greater even than her love for her daughter.

And the shame and the self-hate that came from failing as a mother only pushed her deeper into her addictions, she said, which also made it impossible for her to hold a job, not even stripping, and so to support herself and her expanding drug use, which now included snorting crushed OxyContin, Ines became a working girl, putting ads up on Craigslist.

A few years into that lifestyle, she began to repeatedly attempt suicide, but it was almost like she was too strong to kill, and one time she even jumped in front of a train in the LA subway. A Good Samaritan yanked her out at the last second, but her left foot got sheared off.

None of this, of course, did I know when she asked me to buy her a drink at the Drawing Room. And when I did learn it all during our brief three months together, it didn't stop me from being in love with her. If anything, it made me love her more.

10.

IN THE MORNING I reached out to my friend at the Culver City PD, Gil Sharpe. He works missing persons, and I knew he went in on Saturdays. I tried his cell phone, and he answered after a few rings, which was great. Hardly anybody answers their phone anymore. They haven't for years. But guys like Sharpe still answer.

"Hey, Hank," he said. "It's been a while. How you doing?"

"Good. It's not a big deal, but I'm going by Happy nowadays. No more pretending to be Hank."

Sharpe is a stolid guy, thick-bodied, bald, a lot of black hair on his fingers, but he's always had a compassionate side, an understanding of human nature, which is why he's ended up in missing persons for thirty years. He knows why people get lost and that helps him track them down.

"Okay," he said. "I'll call you Happy. That's not a problem."

"You working?" I knew he was, but I asked anyway.

"Yeah," he said. "What you got for me?"

I gave him the three names and the gist of the situation. Told him that Mary DeAngelo and Hoyt Marrow were the clients, based in LA, and that I wanted some intel on them. Unfortunately, I didn't have their dates of birth, but the girl was twenty-four and the man's age was unknown.

Ines, whose date of birth I could provide, was the person they were looking for, a homeless woman gone missing in or around Olympia. I said I believed she had been arrested recently, and if there was a mug shot of her, I'd appreciate it if he could email it to me.

Sharpe took in all this, then said, "Weren't you involved with a woman named Ines? Years ago? Had a lot of problems?" Befitting his name, Sharpe has a good memory and not much gets past him.

"That's right. The same woman. The daughter, DeAngelo, has hired me to find her."

"So it's a job *and* it's personal?"

"It's a job," I said.

He was silent, wondering if he should counsel me.

Then he decided — at least this is what I was projecting — that I was an adult and knew what I was getting into, which I didn't, because if I did a few lives might have been saved, and he said, "I'll call you back in a little while."

"Thanks," I said, and hung up.

When I was working juvenile in Hollywood, in the late '90s, dealing with a lot of runaways, Sharpe was working missing persons in the same precinct, and, naturally, there was a good deal of overlap between our two departments, and we became friends. Almost fifty-eight now, he's still riding a desk and will have a nice fat pension when he retires. I put in ten years, had an undiagnosed nervous breakdown at the end, and get no pension.

Not able to do much until I heard back from Gil, I took George for a half decent walk, then watered my front yard. The bougainvillea bush quivered noticeably as it drank, it has a lot of personality, and I spoke to the whole yard as I watered, telling everybody — the trees, the flowers, the weeds — that I thought they were beautiful and that I loved them, which I do.

And then I got up close to the bougainvillea with my hose, to soak its roots, and I stared at the little yellow stamens inside the purple flowers. The stamens are not much bigger than a long eyelash, and their yellow heads of pollen are shaped like starfish.

Then I went behind my bungalow, where I have another hose, to do more watering. The back of my house is flush to the wild slope, which is populated with gigantic agave, sprouting their sharklike fins, and the slope goes up about a hundred yards to the tree-covered ridge, where coyotes and bobcats like to stretch their legs. And right behind my house, where I could get at them with the hose, I had planted four trees — two crepe myrtles and two pepper trees.

Each tree was for one of the men I had killed in March of 2019: the organ-transplant doctor, Madvig; the two men who had worked with the doctor, one of whom was his son; and Carl Lusk.

All my killing had been done in self-defense, but that gave me no solace, and so I had planted the trees as a kind of amends and had committed myself to care for those trees every day, to force myself to remember the lives I had taken, and it was around the same time that I planted the trees that I had begun my small study of the Buddha's teachings, the dharma, in addition to my ongoing psychoanalysis, as a way to deal with my guilt for what had happened.

When I went back inside, done watering the living and the dead, Sharpe called and gave me his report. As far as he could tell, Ines wasn't deceased or in prison, but she had been arrested six months ago in Olympia for heroin possession — for the third time, it turned out, which my less-than-stellar website had *not* informed me — and she had been issued a desk warrant. Naturally, she had failed to show up in court, and so if the cops picked her up again, Sharpe figured she'd probably do some time. Then he added, "I remember she was troubled. I guess she still is. Tried to kill herself, right?"

"Yeah. More than once. Her father wrecked her for life. She never could heal from it. You emailed me her mug shot?"

"Yep." Then he told me that he thought Marrow was a phony, coming to the same conclusion I had, and Mary wasn't in the system at all: not even a driver's license. Then, deciding to give some counsel after all, he said, "Maybe you should stay away from this one. Things with junkies never turn out good."

"I need the money, Gil," I said. "And...I guess it is personal. I loved her once. I'd like to find her. Maybe I could help her."

Gil was silent. He knew that you can't really keep people from screwing up their lives. You can only make the suggestion that they *not* screw up, as he had just done, but after that, if they don't want to listen, there's not much you can do. Then he said, "I hope you find her, and things work out good."

"Doesn't hurt to try," I said.

"That's right," he said. Then he sighed, resigned and wise, and switched topics, like nothing else had been discussed. "So other than changing your name, you doing all right? Still got that dog?"

"It's more that I went *back* to my name," I said. "If you see what I mean."

"Okay. What about the dog?"

"I still have the dog. George. We're more in love than ever."

"I wish I had a dog. Send me a picture of him."

"I will. We just came back from a walk."

"That's the life. Anyway, I gotta go. Let me know how it works out."

Then we hung up, and I took a picture of George and sent it to him. He texted back a heart emoji, which surprised me. I didn't expect him to know how to use emojis because I didn't know how to use them, had never needed to, but he inspired me, and I found the things on my phone and texted him a little emoji of a dog.

He responded with another heart, and then I found the hearts, they came in all sorts of colors, and I sent him three hearts — a purple, a red, and an orange — to be funny and creative, but he didn't respond, our little flirtation or whatever it was had come to an end, and then I opened my email in my phone, *that* I knew how to do, and I saw Ines's mug shot, and my real heart, which was already broken, broke some more.

11.

HER SKIN, FROM YEARS of exposure, was dark brown and heavily seamed: lines ran down her caved-in cheeks like thin cuts from a razor. And the way she held her mouth, it seemed that she had lost most of her teeth: she had the clamped-down jaw of the hobo.

And her hair had been sheared off, maybe because of lice, and what was left was an iron-colored stubble, the haircut of a renunciate or a survivor of a death camp.

In the profile shot, her nose was still hawkish and proud, and when she was looking straight into the camera, her eyes, bleached and faded by the sun, were a luminescent light green, especially in contrast to her wood-colored face.

The overall effect was a mask that looked like an old carving on a door or a casket, something to ward off demons, and despite it all, she was still eerily beautiful, but beautiful like a once glorious mansion now ruined, and I put my phone down and found myself crying for the first time since childhood. It was a sensation I had lost all memory of, and it exhausted me, and I went into my bedroom and lay down.

George was at the foot of the bed with some of his toys splayed out in front of him like riches, and I closed my eyes and did some more time travel-ing: I went back to Ines's room that first night after meeting her in the bar, and we're standing next to her bed, kissing. The room is neat and clean, has almost no furniture, and there's a diffused radiance from the streetlamps outside.

Then she steps away from me and sits on her bed and says, "I have something to tell you." Then she removes her shoes and pants, and I see that her left leg, from the knee down, is a flesh-colored prosthesis that looks like half the leg of a mannequin, including a rubber foot with painted red toes. The prosthesis is attached to her knee with an elastic brace, and I recall that when we had been walking earlier, when we left the bar, there had been a slight hitch to her step, but I hadn't thought much of it.

"I lost my foot," she says. "I hope you won't mind."

She then slides off the elastic brace and pulls her footless stump — a shinbone with no muscle — out of the hollow prosthesis, which her stump had fit into like a sheath or a boot.

She holds out her stump for me to see it, and the skin is scarred and flayed, and at the bottom of the stump there seems to be some fleshy padding. "They made a heel for me," she says. "It helps."

"How did this happen?"

"An accident." A few weeks later she will tell me the truth of the "accident."

"I'm very sorry," I say and sit next to her on the bed.

"It happens," she says, with her singsong accent, and then she smiles and laughs, and we start kissing again. She takes off her shirt and her breasts are small and delicate, and then she removes the rubber band holding the long rope of her hair, and she lies back on the bed, her hair fanning out behind her like a cape, and her body is olive-colored, strong, and elegant, despite all her abuses, and later when we make love, I feel pleasure when I come, which had never happened before. A pedophile had broken me when I was a boy — broke something in my mind — and I could never feel anything when I came and didn't know really what I was missing. But something about Ines frees me — maybe because she was even more broken than I was — and afterward I lie next to her and think, *Is this love? Am I in love?*

And we lie there quiet for a while, then she says, "There's something else I have to tell you."

"What?" And I wonder what it could be after the revelation that she's missing a foot, and she's quiet for a moment, then she says, "I'm a working girl, and I need you to pay me. But it doesn't mean I don't like you because I do. Very much."

"You're a prostitute?"

"Yes...It happens."

That, I would learn, was Ines's frequent refrain, her mantra, her response to life. It signaled some kind of profound acceptance and encompassed everything: good things, bad things, the banal, the tragic, and it struck me then as true, and ever since, no matter what occurs, no matter how unexpected, I've often thought, *It happens.*

12.

To come back from the past and clear my head, I smoked a joint and made some coffee. Then I got on my computer and did some more research. There were six hospitals in and around Olympia, and I started making calls. Each place I'd say to the operator some variation of: "Can I speak to Ines Candle? She's a patient but I misplaced her room number."

And none of the places could find her, and so I'd say, "Maybe the emergency room?" And she wouldn't be there, either. Then they'd say, in effect, "She's not in our system," and so I'd thank them and hang up.

Now if I had called and said, "Is there an Ines Candle staying at your hospital?" they wouldn't have told me. But just acting like Ines was already there was a simple bypass of the protocol, and I have done the same sort of thing when I call hotels, trying to hunt somebody down, and every now and then I do get lucky with this technique. But not this time. And it was the same thing with the shelters in Olympia that I found on the internet and called: no sign of Ines.

My conclusion, then, between my calls and what Sharpe told me, was that Ines didn't appear to be hospitalized, incarcerated, or dead. She could have turned up, though, as a Jane Doe at the city morgue, since a lot of homeless don't carry ID, but that was the kind of thing I would have to investigate in person.

I then called Mary DeAngelo — she had put her number in her email — and left a message. She called back right away, and I told her that I hadn't been able to locate her mother and that it did look like I would need to go to Olympia.

"I had a feeling that would be the case," she said. "I'll have my husband's assistant call you in a little while to arrange your travel."

"What about your husband signing off on me first?"

"I told you that was a formality. We'll see you tonight."

Then we hung up, and a half hour later a man named Leland Roscoe, the husband's assistant, reached out to me. I wasn't expecting a man, but that was my bias, and I gave him my date of birth and told him I would like a window seat if possible.

A little while later he called me back and gave me my itinerary for the next day: I had an afternoon flight out of Burbank direct to Seattle, where I'd get a Hertz rental car, and when I made it to Olympia — a ninety-minute drive — I'd have a room waiting for me at the La Quinta Inn.

I then called my friend Rafi, an older man who owns a pawnshop, and asked if he could take George for a few days, and he said he'd love to, which was not unexpected: most people want to spend time with George.

13.

AT 7:50, I MADE a left off Sunset Boulevard into the small, canopied drive-way of the Sunset Tower Hotel, a beautiful 1930s art deco monolith that looks like a spaceship or an Incan temple, depending on your mood.

There were a bunch of Teslas and Jags and Mercedes jammed ahead of me, but then a valet, a young slump-shouldered kid, wearing black pants and a windbreaker, hustled over, and I got out of the car and said, "The keys are in the ignition."

"Okay," he said, and he had an ellipsis of red pimples across his forehead and the equal amount of spacing between each pimple and the next interested me, and I slipped him a twenty. Not because he had bad skin but because I always overtip, especially car jockeys.

He looked at the twenty, smiled at me. "Thanks," he said, with genuine feeling.

"I used to park cars over at Dan Tana's," I said, seizing the goodwill between us. "In the early '90s." That was the job I had between the Navy and the LAPD, and I loved it because you kept moving the whole time and sitting in people's cars was like reading a snippet of their diary, and, best of all, I always had cash in my pocket at the end of the night.

The kid lowered himself into the Chevy and said, like he never heard of it, "Dan Tana's?"

"Yeah, over on Santa Monica. Was a hot spot, like this place now."

He nodded, politely, indifferently, put his hands on the wheel. "Nice car, old-school," he said. Then he inhaled, smelled the weed, and said, "Tasty." Then the door slammed, and he and his pimples drove off with my tank, and I pushed through the glass doors of the hotel and up three marble steps to the lobby.

To the right was the reception desk and a few Swedish-looking chairs that no one probably ever sat in, and to the left was the shadowy interior entrance to the Tower Bar.

There was a couple in front of me at the maître d's lectern and then it was my turn. Behind the lectern was a slender brunette, a composed young woman in a gray tunic, and as I approached, she was glancing down at her reservation book, marking something with a pen, but sensing me, she said, reflexively, without looking up, "Can I help you?"

"Yes, I'm meeting someone. Last name Marrow. A party of two. Now three."

She finished whatever she was doing in her book, looked up at me, and seemed a little surprised. After all, it was Saturday night at the Tower Bar, and I wasn't looking too beautiful. Wasn't all gussied up like most everyone there, smelling good and gleaming good.

Not that I hadn't made an effort.

I had taken an Epsom salts bath, but that hadn't put much of a dent, I realized, in my overall first impression: green-and-purple black eye; nasty facial scar; broken phallic nose, hanging in there until I figured things out; worn-out blue-sponge sport jacket; navy sweater with tiny moth holes; frayed white oxford shirt; well-scuffed ankle boots good for kicking jerks in the shins; and clean khaki pants that nevertheless had a number of coffee stains that I hoped were visible only if you were looking for them.

But Gray Tunic was a professional. She wasn't caught off guard for long, and her face shifted expression from surprise to neutrality — at least I was wearing a jacket — and she said, "What was the name again on the reservation?" And then she gave me a professional half smile, and there was a rather large gap between her front teeth and suddenly I found her very beautiful.

"Hoyt Marrow should be the name on the reservation," I said, and something flashed in her eyes, a private thought, and it seemed like maybe it was an ugly one. Then she said, robotically, "Yes, they're here. Follow me, please."

She came around the lectern, and I had the feeling that maybe she knew Hoyt Marrow — or whatever his name was — and I would have liked to have asked her about him. But this was not the time, and I trailed her into the Tower, a candlelit place for Hollywood players and the pilot fish that surround them, done in soft carpet, wood, and plenty of shadow.

Which meant the lighting was scarce that night, as it would be every night, to hide the tiny scars, and a piano player was making a hash out of something from the American songbook, and women were laughing, and everyone was talking loudly like they had something to say, especially the men, and there was a decadence to the place that gave me a shiver, like feeling that first lurch on the *Titanic*.

But Gray Tunic didn't feel it: she kept a steady clip and piloted me straight to the far-right corner, where Mary and her husband were tucked behind a four-top, sitting side by side in the semidarkness. One little candle flickered on the table, and Gray Tunic said, "Here they are."

Then, without really looking at them, which seemed intentional, she executed a quick pirouette, abandoning me, and Marrow, a very large and broad man, stood up out of the murk, like a water buffalo breaking the surface of a deep pool, and Mary stayed seated.

A sconce on the wall, shoulder level, threw some light on Marrow from below, like in a Dracula movie, and he was wearing a yellow-colored camel hair jacket and an expensive shirt as white as a full moon, and even in those spooky shadows, I could see he'd had a lot of work done.

His nose was too narrow and his chin too manly.

His hair was a row of black plugs sutured into the top of his head, and his pallor was a sleek wood brown, a deep tan meant to signal wealth, but which made me think of Ines sitting outside for five or six years being turned the same color.

His eyebrows had been sculpted into thin, arching dark lines, and I pegged him as fifty trying to look thirty-five and failing terribly. He was as tall as me, six two, but he was much bigger in the chest and arms, from lifting weights and probably from ingesting high-grade testosterone, the kind that rich men can afford; the kind that makes great athletes into gods.

But his brown eyes didn't match his altered looks. I would have expected eyes that were full of delusion and greed and vanity, a glimpse into a hellish emptiness, but these were cold and intelligent eyes, which then became warm, like he had turned them on, and he said, "Mr. Doll?"

"Yes," I said. "Nice to meet you."

"So beautiful to meet *you*," he said, using the world "beautiful" like he was some kind of new-age Hollywood producer; maybe he thought it fit the room. Then he said, "Hoyt Marrow," to keep the introductions going, and he offered me a large, square hand to shake, and he gave me a violent squeeze, the kind that religious zealots or football coaches give, to show you they're real men, men of strength, with an undercurrent of sadism, and I squeezed back, letting him know I was there, but I didn't overdo it and withdrew my hand. I looked down at Mary and she was teething on a champagne glass, not really drinking from it, and I said, "Hello again."

She nodded shyly, and Marrow said, "Please, sit down."

I took the chair across from him, and when he lowered his bulk next to Mary, she looked meek as a child.

He said, "That's quite the black eye you've got."

"Got clipped by the hood of my car," I said and was starting to believe it myself.

Then he motioned to a waiter, who promptly stood by my side. "What would you like to drink?" said Marrow.

The waiter, in his white dinner jacket, bowed his head gracefully at me, and I said, "A child's portion of Don Julio, with ice."

THE WHEEL OF DOLL • 57

"*What?*" said the waiter, more confused and rattled than he should have been, and just a moment earlier he'd been so elegant and deferential.

"Half a shot of Don Julio," I said. "On ice."

This the waiter understood, and he left.

The two of them already had drinks: Mary had her flute of champagne, which she was still chewing on, and Marrow had a whisky. He said to me, smiling, "That's a funny way to order a drink. *A child's portion.*'"

"It's a line I like to use, but it doesn't work too often."

"Why use it at all? Why half a shot?"

"I try to be moderate," I said. "You know, the middle way." Which was a stupid thing to say, spouting off my Eastern notions, when I didn't really know what the hell I was talking about, and after I said it, a sly smile creased Marrow's expensive face, and he put his elbow into Mary's side, gently prodding her. "Another California Buddhist," he said, teasing me and summing me up in the blink of an eye. "Well, you know what they say," he went on. "If you meet the Buddha, *kill him.*"

Then he lifted up his hand, pretending to hold a knife, and made two stabbing motions at me, like he was Tony Perkins. Then, satisfied with his performance, he took a sip of his whisky and smirked at me, thinking himself a great wit, and Mary still hadn't said a word. She just kept her glass at her lips, sucking on it in some sort of regressed state, and she was wearing another old-fashioned dress, with a little bow at the neckline. What she was doing married to this ghoul, I had no idea, though I could guess, and it wasn't a nice guess. Homeless at fifteen might make marriage to Marrow at twenty-four an appealing proposition. Of the worst kind.

The waiter arrived and placed my drink on the table, misting off before I could say thank you, and I picked the tequila up, and the two of them, reflexively, lifted their glasses into the air, and Mary said, breaking her silence, "To finding my mother."

Then we all clinked, and I would have preferred not to, but we looked into each other's eyes, playing that old game of not wanting the curse of seven years of bad sex or whatever it is, though it didn't matter to me, I had been celibate for nearly five years at that point, probably already had the curse, and when I looked into Mary's eyes, one at a time, first the odd left one and then the right, I realized she was wearing contact lenses, which I hadn't noticed in my office, and it looked like she was pinned on some kind of drug—heroin like Ines?—and when I looked into Marrow's eyes, I thought I saw the candle flame dancing in his pupil, but that was just me starting to get hysterical.

Then we all sipped our drinks and Marrow said, "So can we talk business?"

"Of course," I said. This was the part where he looked me over and made sure I was up for the job, even though my ticket was already booked.

"Tell me a little bit about your background," he said. "Your experience."

I outlined for him and Mary, who had gone back to teething on her champagne glass, the general résumé: Navy from eighteen to twenty-five, most of it spent as a master-at-arms, which is a fancy way to say a cop on a boat; ten years in the LAPD, from twenty-five to thirty-five, the bulk of it my tour in juvenile in Hollywood; and sixteen years on my own as a private investigator and now as a security specialist, though I left out the business about losing my license.

"And you've done a lot of missing persons work?" Marrow asked.

I reassured him that I had, both as a cop and as a private operator, and I told them what I had learned so far about Ines from Sharpe, that she had been arrested for heroin possession three times and hadn't shown up in court for her latest offense, which wasn't good — she could go to prison.

This seemed to rouse Mary from her stupor — she was remarkably different from the young woman who had been in my office — and she said, "Would they really put a *sixty*-year-old woman in jail?"

"The prisons need bodies," I said. "All ages welcome."

"Well, it doesn't matter," she said, her voice barely above a whisper, and she was slurring a little. "We're not going to turn her over to the police. Juss want you to find her and put her in a hotel. I looked on the internet. It's in the thirties in Olympia and snowing." Then she slumped back; her little speech had taken a lot out of her.

And I didn't know if the timing was right, but I said, "Did you know that your grandmother died recently? Christmas Day?"

She seemed confused by this, taken aback. She looked at Marrow as if he might understand. Then she said, "What are you talking about?"

I said, "Your grandmother passed."

She thought about this, like she was trying to make sense of it. Then she said, "My father's parents are both dead. A long time."

"I'm talking about your maternal grandmother."

"Oh. I never met her, never even heard anything about her," she said, and she sipped her champagne, then closed her eyes like she was going to go to sleep or pass out.

Marrow said, "How do you know the woman died?"

"The internet. She was in Seattle, in a nursing home. So she wasn't too far from Olympia."

"That's good. You're being thorough," he said. "But it doesn't seem relevant. This woman died on Christmas Day, which I'm sorry about, but Mary's mother has not been heard from since early November."

Mary opened her eyes sluggishly. "That's right."

"Just interesting timing, then," I said, tabling it for the moment, but I sensed a connection, like reaching into a dark closet, groping for the thing you know is there. "Anyway, if I find Ines, I'll tell her. She probably doesn't know."

"Not if. *When*. *When* you find her," said Marrow. "And do you have a winter coat, Mr. Doll?"

Which I took to mean that our "can we talk business" chat had already concluded and that I had passed inspection, and I told him I had a coat that would do, and then Marrow, acting dramatic, like a cliché of a powerful man, suddenly took a folded check and a fat gold pen out of his inside jacket pocket. Everything about him was wrong, lurid.

"I'm going to give you a flat fee of seven thousand dollars," he said, as he

scribbled on the check. "Go up there for a week and see what you can do."
Then he looked up at me. "First name is Happy, right? Happy Doll?"

"Yes, that's the name," I said, and Mary gave a druggy smile, and then
she recited, like it was a nursery rhyme:

"My mother said there was a man named Happy Doll who was a sad
doll and called himself Hank." Then she took a sip of her champagne, finished it, picked up Marrow's drink and finished that—Marrow didn't
seem to care—and I wondered how I could help Mary. Then I thought,
Find Ines first. That's the way.

Marrow handed me the check—it was from City National and didn't
have his name on it; it was the kind you can get from a teller—and I folded
the thing and put it in my pocket.

"Thank you," I said, and Marrow made a gesture to the waiter, who was
walking by, indicating another round for himself and Mary, and I said,
conversationally, "What sort of work do you do, Mr. Marrow?"

He looked at me shrewdly and said, "I don't work. I earned my money
the old-fashioned way. Remember that commercial?" Mary, bored or ready
finally to pass out, closed her eyes again and rested her head on Marrow's
shoulder.

"I do remember that commercial. E.F. Hutton," I said. Marrow and I
were of the same generation. "You're an investor?"

"No, harder work than that. I waited a long time for my parents to die."

"That is hard work."

"The hardest." He smiled wolfishly, then added, "I guess it's your job,
but have you been snooping around about me, Mr. Doll? Why do you want
to know what I do?"

"It's important for me to know who I'm working for."

"You're working for that check in your pocket. And for Mary." Her eyes
flicked open for a moment, then closed again.

"Why do you use a fake name?"

That didn't throw him in the slightest—all his plastic work had given
him a good poker face—and he said, "I come from a very well-known old

family, Mr. Doll, and it affects people poorly when they hear my name. Gives them all sorts of ideas, like extortion and kidnapping and blackmail, and grubby little men like you, private detectives and lawyers and con men, throw themselves at me, and it gets very annoying."

"I imagine it does," I said, though I didn't believe his story for a second.

Then the waiter brought their drinks, and Mary, sensing the waiter's presence, opened her eyes and grabbed her champagne, and Marrow stood and said, "We're going to order dinner now, and I wish you good luck."

I realized, like a slap, he was dismissing me, and so I stood up as well, and Marrow offered me his hand, letting me know he was the bigger man in every way, no hard feelings, and we shook again, and his grip was even more violent this time. Then I looked down at Mary and said, "I'll do my best to find your mother."

"I know you will," she said, drunkenly. "Goodbye, Mr. Doll."

"Goodbye," I said, and I nodded at Marrow as he sat back down.

Then I headed for the lobby, and five steps into the gloom, I snuck a quick glance back, and Marrow had enveloped himself around her, imprisoning her with his arms. Her head was just barely peeking out over his massive shoulder, and even in the darkness, I could see that her eyes were closed in utter surrender and perhaps even bliss.

14.

I RETRIEVED MY CAR and parked it on Sunset about twenty-five yards east of the hotel. Then I walked back toward the Tower and at the edge of the semicircle driveway there was a row of gigantic palm trees. Each tree, swaying high up in the night sky, was at least one hundred feet tall, and I positioned myself behind the first tree in the row. Its round base was as wide as two men, which gave me excellent cover, and I was able to easily keep an eye on the glass doors of the Tower. It was a dull ninety minutes or so, but eventually the two of them emerged. Mary was leaning heavily against her husband, she looked even more blitzed, and they stood there a moment by the valet stand with the other fancy people coming and going.

Then a large black Mercedes SUV, with tinted windows, pulled into the drive, an Uber or a car service, and Marrow helped Mary get in.

I dashed back to my Chevy—you can only make a right out of the hotel driveway—and as I started the car, the Mercedes drove past me on Sunset. I fell in a few cars behind the SUV in the heavy Saturday night traffic, and at Laurel Canyon, they got in the left lane and headed up the dark mountain all the way to the top, where they made a right onto Mulholland Drive.

After a few miles of winding curves on Mulholland, the San Fernando Valley, with its endless grid of light, came into sight far below, and then the SUV made a right onto MacArthur Drive, which steadily climbed and was a street of gated homes surrounded by trees. I stayed back about a quarter mile, then the Mercedes stopped in front of a high black gate, which was sliding open as I drove past.

There was no reason for them to think they were being followed — my headlights would be interpreted as just another rich person heading home on a Saturday night — and I drove a hundred yards up the road and parked.

There were no streetlights — it was very dark out — and as I walked back toward the gate, it began to open again, and I stepped behind a tree along the edge of the street.

Then the Mercedes emerged, made a left onto MacArthur, and headed back toward Hollywood and its next fare. The gate was open for a moment, then started to close, and I could have made a dash to slip in, but I didn't want to risk the driver seeing something in his rearview mirror.

When the Mercedes was out of sight, I stepped out from behind the tree and walked over to the gate, and there didn't appear to be any cameras, and up the driveway, the house, in deep shadow, had just a single light over the front door, and it looked to be one of those single-story, mid-century rectangles, made of white brick. It had a flat roof and there were windows at the front of the house, but they were all dark, and the whole property, which was at least half an acre, sloping upward, with plenty of trees, was surrounded by a black metal fence, like a sylvan fortress.

The neighbors, to the right and left, were fifty yards away, with more trees in between, and there were no houses on the other side of the street: just forest. No cars were coming, and I walked a few feet past the driveway, and by a bunch of pepper trees, I was able to jump up and grab the top bar of the fence, which was about eight feet high.

Calling upon my days as a boxer in the Navy and old muscle memory, I pulled myself up, then swung my right leg over. There were dull black spikes along the top of the fence, and I was straining my arms to keep myself poised above the top bar in order to not be impaled, and I felt like an old fool but then I swung my left leg over, jettisoned myself outward, and landed on the other side, without breaking my ankles, though I did fall as I landed in a large patch of ground ivy.

I stayed there a moment, quiet, waiting to see if I'd be discovered. But I wasn't. Everything was very still and very dark: there was just the one light over the front door and some meager light from a weak half-moon. In the driveway, to the left of the front door, there were three cars parked in front of a two-car garage, and stabbed into the ground by the garage was a private security sign.

Keeping that in mind, I started my way up the sloping yard, staying to the far right, along the perimeter of the property, in the deep shadow of the trees. If there were motion detectors, they would most likely cover the front of the house, near points of access, and not reach the tree line, where too many animals could set things off. And as I got closer, I realized the house wasn't a rectangle, as it presented from the street, but was shaped like the letter L, lying on its side.

I then moved parallel to the bottom of the L, which was a wing of the house with darkened windows, and when I came to the end of the wing, crouching by some bushes, I turned the corner and was now in the backyard, which after all the darkness, exploded with illumination: there was a spectacular blue pool, with underwater lights, and the back of the house was all glass. It was one big, gigantic window, and I could see inside to a brightly lit living room, like looking at the stage of a play.

And starring in the play were four well-built young men, all platinum blondes, sitting on a sectional couch by a large coffee table. On the far wall, on an enormous flat-screen television, highlights of a football game were popping in bright colors, and the young men kept bending over something on the coffee table, and I realized they were taking turns doing lines, probably cocaine, while watching the TV.

Behind the young men, in the background, Mary and her husband were at a drinks cart, and Marrow was making cocktails. Then he and Mary went to the coffee table with their drinks — she seemed a little steadier on her feet now — and they did a line each. After that, they seemed to say good night to the young men and retreated beyond my vision.

I stayed crouched in my hiding spot and watched the platinum blondes — their hair looked dyed — for a few more minutes, without much happening. Then I snuck back around to the front of the house. I took a deep breath and repeated my maneuver by the fence, but badly twisted my right ankle this time, falling hard and tearing my pants at the knee on the asphalt. But no cars came: it was a quiet street of the deeply privileged. I took note of the house number on the mailbox, 1639, then limped back to my car.

15.

AT A STOPLIGHT, on my way home, I texted a friend of mine, Rick Alvarez, and asked him who owned 1639 MacArthur Drive. Rick, in his fifties, trim like a bullfighter, is a licensed realtor and has access to very useful databases. A few years back, I was able to help Rick's elderly father when he got caught up in a senior citizen scam, and ever since, Rick will drop anything for me when I need something. And by the time I was home and walking George on my sore ankle, Rick texted me the name of the owner, Haze Langdon, who, according to the records, had purchased the house back in 1984.

I then googled Langdon, while George sniffed and marked, and Langdon was a Hollywood producer with some big commercial hits in the '80s and '90s, but nothing since. Hollywood was filled with people like this, people who had made a lot of money at one time, bought valuable real estate when it was cheap, then proceeded to hang on for years, waiting to die like the rest of us, but in greater comfort.

There was a recent picture of Langdon at a film opening, and he was a small man, in his seventies, with silver hair, and everything about him was small: he had one of those faces with tiny, perfect features, like a toy person, and he was definitely not the man going by the name Hoyt Marrow.

I then texted Rick and asked him if I could call him, checking first since it was getting late on a Saturday night. His response was to call me, and I answered: "Thanks for getting back to me."

"No problem. What's up?"

"Any way to tell if the owner of this house is renting it or doing an Airbnb?"

"Sure. I can find that out. I'll call you right back."

George and I went another block, and I was pleased to see him begin to defecate. When he was done, I held his offering, in the little poop bag, under the streetlight, and studied it, carefully. To my eyes, it seemed to be well-formed and healthy, indicating no nervous tension or dehydration that I could perceive, and I said, "Good boy, George," and we started walking home, George trotting happily, me limping in my ripped pants.

Then Rick called me back and said, "It doesn't look like he's renting it in any official capacity, and he's not registered for Airbnb, but he could be doing an off-the-books rental. You never know."

"Right," I said.

"You need anything else?"

"No, I appreciate it. How are you? All good?"

"Yeah. You know me. I'm a happy person. I don't know why. Been like this my whole life. Just always feel good."

"That's a blessing," I said.

"I guess." Then I heard his wife call out something in the background, and Rick said, "I gotta go, we're watching a movie. With Paul Newman. *Sweet Bird of Youth.* I haven't seen him in years."

"George likes his canned dog food," I said. "Sometimes I'm tempted to try it myself."

"Newman got involved in all sorts of things. But I better go. She's waiting."

"Thanks for everything, Rick."

"Of course. Anytime, buddy."

An hour later, George and I were in bed, and I was reading *Watership Down,* and George, on top of the covers, by my thigh, was having a dream, vocalizing little yips. He has a rich inner life and may have been dreaming about his nemesis across the street, a proud German shepherd with failing hips named Major.

Meanwhile, I had eaten a cannabis edible before brushing my teeth, to help me sleep when I stopped reading, and I was feeling some far-off paranoia, the usual sense of approaching doom and punishment, but it wasn't too bad. Then, my eyes growing tired, I read this passage in my book:

> *Rabbits (says Mr. Lockley) are like human beings in many ways. One of these is certainly their staunch ability to withstand disaster and to let the stream of their life carry them along, past reaches of terror and loss. They have a certain quality which it would not be accurate to describe as callousness or indifference. It is, rather, a blessedly circumscribed imagination and intuitive feeling that Life is Now.*

I nodded in firm agreement with this, thinking that rabbits were quite wise and that this was an excellent approach to life, something for me to aspire to, and it occurred to me that rabbits were in their own way very Buddhist, since the Buddha preached the utter importance of *the now,* as did all the Eastern philosophies.

Then, too tired to keep reading, I rested the book on my chest and placed my hand, lightly, on George's tawny back: he had stopped yipping and was now sleeping peacefully.

I hadn't intended to disturb him, but the slight pressure of my hand woke him, and he looked at me tenderly and drowsily, and seemed to be saying telepathically, "Don't you think it's time to go to bed?" So I looked at my watch: it was almost 12:30, and he was right. Time for bed.

I turned off the light and George got under the blankets.

He nestled against my right thigh, a good warm spot. My dear pal.

A silvery light from the moon slipped in around the edges of the curtains, and with thoughts of Ines and Mary and the grotesque Marrow swimming around in my mind, I lay there, unable to sleep. I had too many questions: Who were those four young men doing drugs? And why were they in the house? And where did Haze Langdon come in? And who exactly was Marrow?

And as the minutes passed, the edible became more and more amplified in my mind and my body, and I could feel George quite viscerally against my leg, and it seemed like I was having some new level of connection to him, like we were piled up as puppies in a litter together or rabbits in a burrow, and I had a flash of insight, some kind of understanding of why animals sleep so close together, because it felt like George and I were one large fused animal, and what I was experiencing was Darwinian safety in numbers, like a school of fish swimming together to appear like a large fish, and I was *feeling* it ... really feeling it!

And because of this fusing, I began to sense what it was like to be George, to be in his body, to be quick and fast, compact and springy, and he could feel what it was like to be me, ponderous yet strong, and our minds were operating along one pathway, exchanging information, inner blueprints, and I thought, *How could I have never experienced this before?!*

And it was magnificent!

I had always wanted to be a dog!

Or at least part dog!

But then because one is never allowed to stay in heaven for too long, my cell phone rang, like a fire alarm, tragically breaking the spell.

And I cursed the bastard phone! I wanted to be half George again, but it was useless, the moment had passed, maybe never to be felt again, and I reached for the glowing instrument on my bedside table, and there was no name on the screen, only a number, but I pushed ANSWER and it felt strange to speak English after having merged with George, but I managed to spit out: "Hello?"

It was Mary, and her voice was very faint. "I just wanted to thank you again for doing this, Mr. Doll, and also that I'm very sorry about my husband, that he was rude to you."

"You don't have to apologize —"

"But I wanted to."

"I understand. Are you . . . are you all right, Mary?"

"I'm fine. Good night, Mr. Doll." And she abruptly hung up.

Like everything to do with this case, her call was strange and disconcerting, and I thought of calling her back, but I didn't, and I put the phone down on the table.

Then I closed my eyes and thought about the trip ahead and wondered if I might really find Ines and what that would be like, and George was still warm against my leg, peacefully oblivious to my problems, and I dreaded parting from him the next day.

PART II

1.

BY THE TIME I got into Olympia Sunday night, it was too late to do anything, but Monday got off to a half decent start. I was at the county coroner's office by 9:30 and slipped a clerk, a skinny guy on a smoke break, a hundred dollars.

I waited outside for him — a light snow was falling — and I thought he might stand me up, but then he came back out and told me that no sixty-year-old Jane Does, missing a left foot, had shown up in the last two months, which was good news and made me feel productive.

My next step was to start canvassing shelters and soup kitchens that I had looked up on the internet, and the first few places didn't yield anything. I had printed up Ines's mug shot and told people — the workers and the indigent — that I was searching for Ines on behalf of her daughter, but nobody recognized her.

Around midday, a nice older woman in her seventies, a volunteer at a church soup kitchen, did give me some very helpful information, and the productive feeling from the morning, which would be short-lived, flared back up.

Her name was Claire, and she wore her gray hair in youthful hippie braids. She was intrigued by my story of Mary looking for her mother, and while she didn't recognize Ines when I showed her the printout, she offered to sit down with me and tell me what she knew about the world of the homeless in Olympia. She considered herself — after several years of volunteer work — to be an expert on the situation and got us situated in the basement of the church, both of us with coffees in thin paper cups.

There was children's artwork on the walls of the room — leftover Christmas drawings — and the room was chilly. Claire was wearing a down ski vest over a white cabled sweater, and I kept my wool overcoat on. We were sitting at a long folding table, the kind popular in churches for Bible classes and AA meetings. "Thank you for talking with me," I said.

"I'm happy to," she said, and I saw her sneak a glance at my scar and then look away. "Well, the first thing you should know," she said, looking a little over my shoulder to avoid the scar, "is that it's getting really bad here with the homeless, like all over the country."

"In LA, it's a tragedy what's happening."

"So I've heard, and we don't have your weather, but we still have about a thousand homeless now, which is almost double in the last three years."

"What's the overall population of the city?"

"About fifty thousand. So almost two percent are now living on the street. And we have about thirty or so encampments, spread all around. We go to them sometimes and bring blankets and food and even clean needles. Some encampments are bigger than others. And the way the people live, it's terrible. I grew up in this city. It's been like watching someone die."

"At least you do something about it."

"Does feel hopeless sometimes... What keeps you going?"

I showed her a picture of George on my phone as my answer and that made her laugh; then I said to her, "Could you tell me where these encampments are?"

She started giving me the locations — the highway overpasses, the parks, the abandoned rail yards, the streets where people lived in their cars — and I wrote it all down in my little notebook.

After that there wasn't really much more she could tell me — except to give me the addresses of a few soup kitchens that I hadn't found on the internet — and I thanked her for her time and made a donation to the church. As we parted, she said, "I hope you find this woman and get her off the street, but you know a lot of them don't want to come indoors. They get accustomed to that life and it's hard for them to change. But maybe she'll be different."

"I hope so."

For the next four days, using a AAA map as my guide, I started in the northeastern part of the city, with La Quinta as my starting point, and worked my way south and eventually west. I'd drive my rental car to a neighborhood, then make my way on foot. After snow on the first day there was intermittent rain, and despite the cold, wet weather, my twisted ankle got a little better each day.

The city, which was about twenty square miles, was divided into east and west by two good-size bodies of water: Budd Inlet and the man-made Capitol Lake. Once I got to the west side, my plan was to then work my way back north and then east again, making a circle. If this method didn't turn up Ines, I'd expand the radius, as I heard there were encampments in the communities surrounding the capitol, like in a town called Tumwater.

Under less dreary circumstances, I might have found Olympia, the capital of the state, beautiful. Of course, it had the usual American ugliness — 7-Elevens and invasive highways built through old neighborhoods — but there were also plenty of fir trees, some nicely made governmental buildings, and a sense of the past with a downtown area that still had some life. There was also a marina with hibernating boats, their unsheathed masts like lances poking at the sky. And the whole town was built around the tail end of the Puget Sound, the last place the Pacific could reach on its inland journey, with fingers of water everywhere.

But the scrim over my eyes — the depressing task at hand and a growing sense of futility — made everything ugly. And wherever I went in the wintry-wet city, Mount Rainier loomed on the horizon, like an angry god made of rock and ice. One positive was that I wasn't smoking weed or having any tequila. I could have gone to a marijuana store or stopped in a bar, but I wanted to stay clear and receptive while I searched for Ines, and I thought that when I got back to LA, I would keep this up. If I was really serious about my Buddhist inclinations and making another leap of growth in my analysis, it was time to stop dulling my mind.

By Thursday, I had hit almost all the shelters and soup kitchens, with no leads, and had gotten halfway through the list of camps that Claire had told me about. I had shown the printout to at least 150 homeless people, men and women of all ages and races, and they were all in rough shape, cold and dirty. Many of them were insane or drug addicted or both, though not all of course. Some were just broke, really broke.

And I despaired for the people I met, for the way they had to live, and as a discipline I tried to do tonglen with their pain, breathing it in, imagining it, taking it on, and then as I exhaled, I'd send them well-being and even love.

And in the more practical realm, I gave most everybody I met five dollars for talking to me, if they wanted it, which not everybody did. Some people were prideful that way.

I kept Mary DeAngelo apprised of my progress, or, rather, lack of progress, texting her once a day, and I was hoping, of course, as I went to the shelters and the camps, to get a lead on Ines or even better just stumble across her, but I didn't have that kind of luck.

What made things especially difficult was that the homeless people I spoke to didn't respond well to my presentation of Ines's mug shot. They were all wary of being a snitch, even though I assured them I wasn't a cop. But it didn't matter — if they knew Ines, they weren't telling me, or they genuinely had no idea who she was.

Another obstacle was that I didn't have a lot of hours of daylight to work with: the sun went down each day around 4:30, the temperature would drop from the forties to the low thirties, and people didn't want to come out of their warm tents, after dark, to talk to me.

Which did give me plenty of time in my room at La Quinta.

Which also meant plenty of time to think about Ines and our relationship back in 2007. It was painful to recall, but after she told me she was a working girl, I made an arrangement with her: I'd give her fifteen hundred bucks a month to take down her ad on Craigslist and to give it a go just with me.

She accepted the deal, and this wasn't sane behavior on my part, but I wasn't a picture of mental health at that time or any time. My mother died giving birth to me, a pedophile wrecked me when I was thirteen, and my father, who always resented me for sending my mother to the grave, died of alcoholism when I was eighteen. And all this set me up to really want to save Ines when I met her.

Couldn't save my mom.

Couldn't save my dad.

But Ines would be the one!

Of course it was me I needed to save, but at thirty-eight I hadn't learned that yet. That didn't happen until I was forty-six when I showed up at Dr. Lavich's, who was part of an institute that saw ex-cops and ex-military for free.

But long before I got on the couch, I had my three months of madness with Ines. I was able to get her to stop being a working girl but I couldn't get her off drugs and so I did them with her. One time, we snorted Oxy-Contin, and I didn't see the appeal at all. It was like being hit with a mallet right in your brain and about ten minutes after we did a few lines, Ines and I both passed out. One moment I was awake, feeling numb and strange, and then I was gone.

I didn't wake up for six hours and when I came to my right arm was like a thick rubber hose at the end of my shoulder that I could swing but not control. I had passed out in an awkward position — the Oxy kept me from waking up and shifting — and I had compressed a nerve and the thing wasn't right for a week.

We also, a few times, snorted some hideous cocaine, but that was always, even before Ines, my least favorite drug. Back in the day, I never used to turn it down, but I would also never seek it out because it always made me feel like a dumb rat going back to the dropper in some experiment. Sure, the first line, you feel like a movie star, but after that all you do is swivel your jaw like a crackhead, and yet you don't stop, you chase that movie-star feeling all night long without ever tasting it again, and you become like that character in the Richard Pryor bit who's always saying, "Where can I get some more? Where can I get some more?"

But the main drug that Ines loved and pursued was heroin. She'd shoot it in her good foot — her only foot — and a few times when she shot up, I snorted it to keep her company.

She didn't want me to try the needle — in her own way she was trying to protect me — but even snorting it, I never felt anything so beautiful in my life.

I'd get the powder up my nose, close my eyes, wait for it, and then suddenly my mind would explode with a gold light, like a glimpse of the sun without being burned, and I'd become aware of the utter absence of pain, which was like a glimpse of heaven.

Then as it wore off, I'd fall into a kind of gentle slumber, the kind I imagine a baby might feel in its mother's arms, a feeling I never knew.

But then later, I'd be all jangly and lost and frightened, and after the gold light the world would be leached of color, like a black-and-white anxious dream, and after three or four times snorting it, despite the lure of the gold explosion, I somehow had the strength to never do it again. I didn't necessarily feel like I had much to lose, but what little I had I knew that heroin would take.

So maybe Ines was barely present with all that shit in her system, but what she could give me when she *was* present felt like love to me. I didn't feel ashamed around her, I didn't feel secretly ugly like I did with other people, and it was crazy, of course, but I felt safe with her, like she would never hurt me, and until I experienced that with Ines, I realized I had never felt that way with anybody.

She could also be morbidly funny, said if she ever got onstage and talked about her life, she'd call it "stand-up tragedy." One time, she said, practicing her imagined routine, "I've been an acrobat, a stripper, and a hooker—nobody's had my career!"

And every night, as a kind of ritual, after she took off her prosthesis and had gotten into bed, she'd say, "Hank, would you mind getting me a glass of water? I'm all disassembled."

Maybe it was me, but she made me laugh, and when we'd stand on her roof, looking out over LA, watching the sky turn purple, I'd step back and look at her and just marvel. She was so magnificent and strange—her gigantic mane of black hair streaked with iron, the light green eyes, the hawklike profile. And in bed, she fit in my arms like a gift, like a second heart, and with her face hidden in my neck, she'd say, "I love you, Hank. You're very special and very beautiful."

And maybe it was all clichés, but because *she* said it and had seen so much of life, I believed it, and in the beginning, all smitten and crazy and worshipful, I felt like she must be half animal, that she had an animal's strength and an animal's wisdom to abide anything, to seemingly accept everything with her philosophy of "it happens."

But then this other side began to emerge.

She linked it to her period, which at forty-seven she was still getting, and so once a month, a dark curtain she said would come down over her and a voice would tell her it was time to go, that she really had to go, that she had to be erased for all the bad things she had done.

And it was always right before her period, in our three months together, that she would try to kill herself: twice with pills, with me taking her to the ER both times, and then the time in the tub, when she opened up her arms, after which she left LA, and I thought I'd never see her again.

But then on Friday afternoon, thirteen years later, on my fifth day in Olympia, I found her.

2.

I WAS LED TO HER by an old man who was sitting in the back of his rusted green van. The back doors of the van were open like wings, and he sat on the lip of the interior, with his feet dangling. Behind him was his mattress, and there was clutter and garbage all around his bed, like a human version of a bird's nest — if the bird had begun to lose its mind.

It was nearly 4:30 — the sun was getting close to setting — and I was on a street, Deschutes Parkway, that Claire had told me about: people could live in their cars there without being hassled by the cops.

Deschutes ran along the west side of Capitol Lake, which was about two miles around, and the water was pewter gray that late afternoon, reflecting the pewter sky. There were at least thirty vehicles parked on the street: RVs, small campers, cars, pickup trucks. All of them beat-up and battered. I had spoken to about half the inhabitants, when I approached the man sitting in the back of his van.

He was wearing a heavily soiled down winter coat and dirty blue pants. He was short, maybe five five, and his feet, in thick, shiny black boots, didn't quite reach the ground from his perch. He had grizzled stubble on his bullet-shaped head, gray, baggy jowls, and a fleshy, half dead nose, almost purple in color — the pickled nose of an alcoholic.

In his mouth was a stub of a cigar and in his hand was a shiny black leather hat, the kind with earflaps. He was working on the hat, rubbing it with a rag, and in his lap was a can, like a tobacco can, with a waxy yellow substance inside. He dipped the rag into the can and rubbed the substance onto the hat, taking great pleasure in his work.

As I walked up to him, I said, "What are you working on there?"

He looked up at me. His eyes were teary and blue, and the lids were a sickly pink. He took the cigar stub out of his mouth. "What did you say, young man?"

"What have you got there?" I indicated the can in his lap.

The question pleased him, and he smiled at me, and the brown roots of his teeth were all exposed. He said, "Saddle soap. Best stuff in the world." He pointed to his black boots. "You rub it into your boots and when they get wet you see little soap bubbles on the toes. Then you know that your shoes are waterproofed, and you don't need to wear rubbers."

"That sounds good," I said.

"Yes, it's important to keep your feet dry in this town, and when you see the little bubbles you know you're all set. That's why cowboys use it. For their saddles. Saddle soap. See?" He was very voluble on the subject, and I thought this was another dead end, but I kept the conversation going.

"And it's good for your hat, too?"

"Oh, yeah. When it snows, I pull the flaps down and the snow goes on the flaps, but it's waterproof because of the saddle soap, you see. That's why the state troopers wear these hats. For the flaps. And when it stops snowing, I put the flaps up and there's iron snaps and you can hear 'em." He snapped the flaps into place to demonstrate the sound.

"How long have you had that hat?"

"So long I haven't thought about it."

"I should get some saddle soap. My boots are all wet." And they were, from walking in the rain and the gray leftover slush of snow for five days.

"Well, you can get this stuff at the hardware store. When you buy three cans, there's no tax, and you don't run out. So just go to the hardware store — there's one on the other side of the lake, and a few blocks over, called Ace." He pointed across the large lake. "You can find it there and on the bottom of the can, in simple words, they tell you how to use it." He turned the can over to show me. "Then you'll be all set and you won't have to wear rubbers. And on the side is a latch, like a propellor, and that's how you open it." He showed me the latch.

"I really appreciate you telling me all this. Can I ask you a question?"

"About saddle soap? They call it saddle soap because of cowboys."

"No, something else." I showed him the printout of Ines, which was very creased from being folded and refolded. "Have you seen this woman? I'm looking for her."

"Is she a felon? What she do? Rob a bank?"

"No. Drugs."

"Needle drugs?"

"Yes."

"Can I see that?" I handed him the printout and he studied it. "You know, I think I know her. I notice women. Been a while but I think I used to see her panhandling at Ralph's supermarket, which is where I go. Not to panhandle but to shop. And if she's a druggie, they're all under the bridge together. They call it the junkyard."

"Why do they call it that?"

"Because they're all junkies."

"And what bridge is that?"

"Fourth Avenue Bridge. Just up the road two miles. Same bridge you take to Ace for the saddle soap. And to the Ralph's."

I checked my little notebook for the places Claire had told me about and pulled out the map: under the bridge was one of the encampments I hadn't hit yet. I showed him the map, pointed at the Fourth Avenue Bridge. "Definitely this bridge?"

"That's the one."

My heart began to pound: I could feel that I was on the verge of finding her. "Can I give you some money for this information?" I didn't want to presume.

"Sure. I always need money. Gas. Food. Wine. It's all my stomach can handle now, you see. Used to be a vodka drinker, but those days, like my women days, are over."

Feeling like the case was about to break, I gave him a hundred for good luck. He stared at the bill. "This is very generous of you." And he pocketed the money fast before it might be taken away.

"I'm going to head over there now," I said. "I've been looking for her all week. Thank you, sir, for your help."

I offered my hand, and he gave me his hand, which was leathery and cold but still strong. Then I started to walk off and he called out to me. "It's getting dark." He looked up at the sky. "Be careful over there. That's a rough group. They don't like outsiders and they don't like cops. Because of the drugs. Are you a cop?"

"I used to be."

"I thought so."

I nodded and walked quickly back to my car, and it occurred to me I hadn't gotten the man's name.

3.

NIGHT WAS COMING ON FAST, and I pulled over by the bridge, which was made of concrete and quite tall, and it was about a quarter mile long, spanning Capitol Lake down below.

On the bridge were a series of streetlamps, glowing in the gray, dusky light, and underneath the bridge — roughly thirty yards away, down a muddy embankment — I could make out tents and campfires and a few people milling about.

The bridge provided a roof for the camp, cover from the rain and snow, and this was where the Deschutes River fed into the lake. I could see that there was a strong current in the darkening water, and I watched the people going about their business down below and thought about what the old man had said.

So I drove across the bridge and went to Ace Hardware. I hadn't been able to take my baton on the plane with me in my carry-on luggage, but at the hardware store I picked up a thick fourteen-inch Maglite, which, when I loaded it with batteries, was good and heavy, a real club that fit nicely in my hand, and the thing would serve two purposes: illumination and defense, if I needed it.

And for the hell of it, I also picked up a tin of saddle soap.

Then I drove back across the bridge, and it was fully dark now. I parked on the side of the road, climbed over a metal guardrail, and made my way down the sloping well-trod path in the half frozen mud.

I kept the flashlight off — the lamps on the tall bridge gave me enough light to see by — and as I made my way down the slope, I could hear some kind of commotion coming from beneath the bridge, shouts punctuated by screams of pain.

When I got to the bottom, the camp was to the left, under the vaulted arch of the bridge, and the camp was as wide as the four-lane bridge above it and about twenty yards long, crowded with tents and other makeshift structures, right up to the water's edge.

There were a few small campfires, which I had been able to spot from the road, and in the center of the camp two larger fires burned in rusted metal barrels.

And by the barrels was the source of the noises I had heard: three men stood over a man on the ground, and they were kicking him, taking turns, and the man on the ground was turtled up, trying to protect himself. About a dozen people stood in the glow of the fires, watching.

I got closer but was still on the edge of the camp, and I saw that the three men were skinhead types, pale-faced boys, maybe in their early twenties, and the man on the ground was a Black man, and when his face peeped out for a moment, he looked much older than the boys, maybe in his sixties, and the skinheads, between kicks, were taunting him.

"No holding out on us, old man!"

"You fuck us! We fuck you!"

Then one of them looked at the crowd and shouted, "See, this is what you get!"

Then the three of them each kicked the man savagely at the same time, and he grunted and cried out, and I closed the distance, came into the firelight. I removed the heavy flashlight from my overcoat pocket, like a truncheon, and shouted, loudly, "WHAT THE FUCK IS GOING ON HERE?"

First thing I had learned as a cop in the Navy was to be loud, very loud. It's a psychological thing, and the three skinheads all looked up at me and so did their audience.

Then the three of them stepped around the Black man and came toward me, which was good: at least they had stopped kicking him.

There were two tall ones, about six feet, and a midsize one, and they were dressed alike: shit-kicker boots, dirty jeans, and greasy down winter coats with hoodies underneath. Their heads were stubbly, with lots of scabs, and one of the tall ones had face tats, groupings of little skulls on his forehead and his cheeks, and he must have been the leader, because he shouted back at me, "WHO THE FUCK ARE YOU?"

And on cue, a switchblade appeared in his right hand and the other two seeing that brought out *their* weapons: the midsize one had a switchblade like the leader and the other tall one had a box cutter. They were set up in an arrow formation with Skull Tats at the front, and we were about six feet apart.

"I'm a cop," I said. "Go crawl into your tents and leave the old man alone."

"You're not a fucking cop," said Skull Tats, and he fearlessly took a step toward me, knife out — *this was his territory* — and he was about to attack, and so I knelt down fast, scooped up some dirt, threw it in his face, charged him, and clubbed him in the neck with the Maglite, and he went down at my feet.

I then kicked him hard in the stomach, and he stayed down, and then the other tall one went to slash me with the box cutter. I jumped back, the razor whistling by my face, and then the midsize one with the switchblade tackled me — they were smart, coming at me at the same time — and his arms went around my waist. Then with his right hand he was trying to stab me through my wool overcoat but wasn't able to get through the thick material, and so he stabbed me in the thigh, and it hurt like hell, and I was stumbling backward, with him attached to me, and he stabbed me again, but he was at least making it hard for Box Cutter to cut me, and before he could stab me again, I brought the Maglite down hard on the point of his head and he screamed and slid off me, and then it was just me and Box Cutter and he was slashing at me wildly, and I timed it right and knocked the cutter from his hand, then slammed him hard on his shoulder, and he fell to the ground, kneeling in front of me, and I kicked him in the jaw and he went flat, but then Skull Tats got to his feet and charged me, and I swung the Maglite to fend him off, caught him in the side of the neck again, and down he went.

Now all three were on the ground, writhing, mewling in pain, but, thankfully, not dead. I gave each of them a solid kick in the stomach to keep them down, and almost fell to my knees, twanging with adrenaline, but managed to stay on my feet. I then took a few deep breaths, and a calm came over me and I was once more of this world.

My vision during the fight had been primitive, red-hued, like the vision of a lizard, and I'd had no real sense of hearing, but now suddenly, like some beautiful moment post-meditation, I could hear the breeze and feel the chill in the air. I could see that the streetlamps on the bridge high above were reflected on the water of the lake, shimmering like candles, and all around me was my ragtag audience of about a dozen lost souls, their faces ghoulish and medieval in the firelight.

The three skinheads didn't seem to have any allies in this group or at least none willing to mess with me, and the Black man was gone, had crawled off somewhere. One young guy, not a skinhead, but maybe wanting the skinheads to hear, said, "Get out of here, we don't want you here," but he stepped backward as he said it.

I felt my thigh: it was bleeding pretty good and my hand, when I brought it up, was red with blood. Liking the drama of it, I lifted my bloody hand and said to them, like hailing a wild tribe, "I'm looking for a woman named Ines Candle. One hundred dollars to the person who can tell me where she is!"

There seemed to be recognition on all their faces, and then a skinny young white woman in a dirty parka, who had deep purple hollows under her eyes and cheeks ravaged by acne scars, said, "I know Ines. We all know Ines. She's in her tent."

I glanced at the skinheads. They were starting to rouse a little and were glaring at me, but I didn't think they'd give me any more trouble. I took the hundred out of my wallet and said to the young woman, "Bring me to her, please."

She took the hundred, looked nervously at the three men on the ground, then started walking toward the water, indicating that I should follow her. And I did.

4.

INES'S LITTLE PUP TENT, which also had a blue tarp of some kind draped over it, probably for insulation, was about ten feet from the water and right next to an enormous concrete stanchion for the bridge. It was darker over here, no little campfires, and I put the Maglite on. Next to the tent was a battered wheelchair and scratchy radio music was coming out of the tiny shelter. It was a famous Fleetwood Mac song that I couldn't remember the name of, but I could never forget Stevie Nicks's voice, which I had always loved, and she was singing: "Players only love you when they're playing."

The tent was zippered closed from the inside and the young woman bent down by the zipper and said, "Ines, there's a man here for you. He just beat up three of the sick boys. Said he's here to see you."

A voice, that maybe sounded like Ines, said, "What?" Then the radio was turned off.

"A man is here for you. He beat up some of the sick boys." That trio had a fitting name. And that was just *some* of them? I looked over my shoulder. Nobody approached.

The voice from the tent said, "Who beat up the sick boys?"

I said, "Ines. It's Hank. Hank Doll from LA. Your daughter sent me to find you. Come out of the tent."

"Hank?"

"Yeah. Come out. Let me see you."

"I can't come out so easy. You come in."

The zipper came down and I got on my knees; the stab wounds started to hurt bad, and I realized my adrenaline was wearing off. I poked my head into the mouth of the tent and was blinded by a flashlight beam, and I shielded my eyes.

"Oh, my God, Hank, what happened to your face? That's a scary-looking scar."

"Lower the light, I can't see."

She held the flashlight on the floor of the tent like a torch, its beam going straight up, and my eyes adjusted and there she was. She was in a sleeping bag, facing me, propped up on an elbow, and she was swaddled in an old green sweater and a dirty Seattle Seahawks knit cap was on her head. She smiled brightly at me, just a few teeth on the bottom, and she looked both ancient and like a baby. Her eyes, so bleached by exposure, were a pale green that was almost phosphorescent, and a mix of smells came out of the tent: cigarette smoke, urine, feces, and something sour I couldn't place but it wasn't good.

I said, "Hello, Ines."

"You've changed a lot," she said.

I had changed a lot!

"You look the same," I said, and we both laughed, and it was like no time had passed since I'd seen her last. With some people it's like that — right back into the groove of the record. And maybe that's why she didn't seem at all surprised to see me there, kneeling in the dirt, and my first impression of her in that moment was that she was sort of merry, the way a person might be at the beginning of dementia or if they were on drugs. And in Ines's case I suspected both. She seemed high and living on the street was like dog years: Ines was sixty but in street years, it was more like she was eighty. She very well could have dementia.

The girl bent down, interjected, "Ines, he beat the shit out of Scruggs and Willie and Pike because they were giving Samuel a beat-down."

"What did Samuel do?"

"His son gave him some money," the girl said, "and they found out."

"Oh, shit."

"Don't worry about that right now, Ines," I said. "Your daughter sent me to find you. I've got a hotel room. I want to take you there, get you out of here."

"What hotel?"

"La Quinta Inn."

She looked at me a moment, quiet, considering, then: "Could I take a bath?"

"Definitely."

"Okay, I'll go then. But I have a situation."

"What?"

She unzipped her sleeping bag and said, smiling, "I'm half the woman I used to be."

Then she put her flashlight beam on her legs, which were no longer legs: beneath the green sweater was a pair of gray sweatpants, tied off at the bottom, maybe a foot from her hips. "I got gangrene in my stump *and* in my good leg and they double-amputated me, six inches above both knees. It started with the toes on my good foot a couple of months ago, then it all went bad. Happens to a lot of us out here. A lot of gangrene. From frostbite. They chop you up until there's nothing left."

I thought about the old man saying you needed to keep your feet dry in this town. "When did this happen?"

"A month or two ago. I don't know. Hard to keep track of time when you lose so much of your body. I think I've only been out of the hospital maybe two weeks."

The girl said, "Yeah, about two weeks. A few days after Christmas."

"I'm so sorry about this, Ines."

"It's okay." She smiled toothlessly. "It happens."

There it was: the old refrain. She grabbed a coat and a full, dirty backpack, and tossed them out of the tent. Then she passed me her radio, her flashlight, her dirty sleeping bag, a blanket, a little clear plastic bag with two crumpled cigarette packs, a lighter, and a lot of half smoked butts that looked like they'd been found on the street, and the last item was another plastic bag with a can opener, several cans of beans, and a bunch of sardine tins — we had a similar diet. Then using her arms, she crawled out. "Can you put me in my chair?"

I lifted her up — she was as light as a child — and placed her in the wheelchair. Behind the chair, draping from the handles, was a black garbage bag.

"And put all that stuff in the bag." She indicated her possessions.

"Do you need all this?"

"Yes. If I leave it, everything will get stolen. Right, Tracy?"

The girl nodded, and she helped Ines put on her soiled winter jacket. I figured it was easier to do what Ines said, and I rolled up the sleeping bag and put everything in the big garbage bag, except for the blanket, which Ines kept in her lap.

"Don't forget my backpack," she said. "I have stuff in there. Can you wear it?"

I adjusted the straps and got the dirty backpack on. Then I started pushing Ines in the chair through the camp: the earth was just hard-packed enough to make it possible, though there was garbage strewn everywhere. The girl, Tracy, trailed along with us and a couple of people came out of their tents, watched us go by. One of them, another ravaged, emaciated white girl, said, "Where you going, Ines?"

Ines jerked her thumb back at me, said proudly, "La Quinta hotel for a bath. This is my old boyfriend. His name is Hank Doll, but it's really Happy Doll, if you can believe it."

I didn't bother telling her about my going by Happy now, that could wait, and we went past the fires in the rusted barrels and the sick boys were gone. When we got to the bottom of the slope, she said, "What we do here is, you let me hold on to your neck. It'll make it easier to push the chair. That's what we do when we go into town."

Tracy said, "I can push the chair, if you want. Ines is like my momma."

"That's right, baby," said Ines.

"Okay," I said, and I let the girl take the chair, and I lifted Ines and she wrapped her arms around my neck and hung on to me. About halfway up the slope, Skull Tats appeared at the bottom and shouted, "Tracy come back here or I'm going to beat your ass!"

The girl looked frightened, handed me the chair to push, and ran back down the slope. She swerved past Skull Tats and he took a swing at her and missed, and she disappeared into the camp.

"You better not hurt her!" I screamed.

"Fuck you! You can come back down if you want, asshole. Go another round." The other two sick boys joined him. They didn't look so eager, but neither was I. Skull Tats waved his knife at me, a glint of light.

"We better go, Hank," Ines said. "Tracy will be okay. She knows how to handle him."

I started pushing the chair the rest of the way up the hill, and Skull Tats shouted after us, "Don't ever come back here, Ines! You do and I'll kill you!"

Ines twisted violently in my arms.

"Fuck you, Scruggs!" she shouted, and I knew that she was half performing, needing to save face, and Skull Tats — *Scruggs* — gave us the finger. Then he and the other two walked back into the camp.

I labored the rest of the way up the slope, got Ines into the front seat, then folded her wheelchair and put it in the trunk. When I sat behind the wheel I felt bad doing it but I lowered my window a little because of the smell coming off her, and said, "Who are those sick boys?"

"They run the camp," she said.

"What do you mean they run it?"

"We give 'em our money and they provide the drugs."

"What money?"

"Whatever we panhandle we have to give to them, and if you have an ATM card you hand it over. Like I get disability every month, eight hundred dollars, goes right into the bank, but I never see it because they have my card."

"Why are they called sick boys?"

"Because they're sick, sick in the head, and if you don't do what they say, they beat you up or they won't fix you, which is worse."

"That one Scruggs is the leader?"

"No. This big guy is. The Fat Man. He has filed teeth."

I let the filed teeth part alone, but said, "*The* fat man?"

"Yeah. That's how I know him. He runs a couple of junkyards. That's what they call this place. A junkyard. But it's not a bad setup. Everything you need is right here."

"Are you high right now, Ines?"

"No, no money, no funny."

"What's that mean?"

"I don't have the money to get high. I get my disability the fifteenth and Scruggs only gives me enough for about two weeks. After that I go on methadone. But I don't mind the methadone. I had some this afternoon. Gives you a good feeling. You drink it. Have you ever had it?"

"No."

"It lasts a real long time, like a twenty-four-hour martini."

Then she laughed merrily, and it struck me how transformed she was, that she was completely of that place. Then she squeezed my hand, telling me with her eyes that she was happy to see me, and I felt a profound tenderness for her and with the back of my fingers, I touched her cheek gently, and she smiled at me, and behind that smile, amid the ruins, I could see the Ines of thirteen years ago.

Then she said, "So my daughter, Mary, sent you for me?"

"Yeah. She doesn't want you living like this anymore."

"I'm still going to need my fix."

"I know...Let me call her right now." I tried Mary and it went right to voice mail, which was full. So I sent her a text message: Found your mother. She's with me, safe. Call us. It was a little after 5:30. It had been exactly one week, almost to the minute, that I had first met Mary, and the circularity of this appealed to me.

Then I started the car and on the way to the hotel, I stopped at a CVS to get some ointment and bandages for my leg. I had covered the seat in blood.

5.

MY ROOM AT LA QUINTA was on the ground floor and we used the unlocked side entrance off the parking lot, bypassing the lobby. When we got to the room — two queen beds, cheap furniture — Ines marveled at its glamour.

"This is so beautiful, Hank," she said as I wheeled her in.

"I'm actually going by Happy these days."

"Finally. I always thought that was a great name. *Happy Doll.* Like something you could play with."

I smiled and went to the bathroom to bandage my leg. The wounds had coagulated, but they didn't look good. I figured that after I got Ines settled, I'd go to the ER.

When I came out, Ines, sitting patiently in her wheelchair, was staring out the window at the back of the hotel: it had begun to snow. I said, "Are you hungry?"

"Yes."

"We could order something. What would you like?"

"Chinese food," she said, without hesitation. "Wonton soup, lo mein noodles."

"Perfect. How about a bath first and then we order food?"

"That sounds good."

She handed me her winter coat and Seahawks hat — her hair, like in the mug shot, was a shorn gray stubble — and I put all her belongings in the closet. Everything had a bad odor and was making me neurotic. Then I lifted her out of the chair and placed her on the bed I wasn't using, to make it easier for her to undress, and she said, as she began to wriggle out of her sweatpants, "You've seen it all. I have no shame."

But I hadn't seen it all, not like this, and it was hard for her to balance, sitting on the soft bed with her stumps, and she fell onto her back. This made her laugh, and she said, "Help me," and she stayed on her back, like a baby ready to be changed, and as I undressed her, it was hard not to cry at what she had done to herself.

Her legs had been reduced to short, swollen tubes of flesh, and at the bottom of each stump was a vivid scar left by her stitches: vertical red lines, cross-hatched with one long horizontal line, like a drawing of a fence. And the scars were a terrible reminder, a clear demarcation on each leg where the medical saw had done its work.

Her arms were also brutalized, but in a different way. The skin from wrist to elbow, on both arms, was punctuated with small brown bruises, some of them festering, and beneath the surface, I could see her gray-colored dead veins, like dried-out streams, and also faint now, like long white scratches, were the scars from when she had opened her arms all those years ago.

Remarkably, her torso was still beautiful, seemingly untouched by time, though she did have a severe farmer's tan: from years of exposure, her neck and face were cooked a dark brown, while her chest and belly were yellow-brown.

When she was completely naked, I put the coverlet over her, stashed her dirty clothing in the closet, and told her to wait while I got the bath ready, which was the first thing I should have done. But the tub filled quickly, and I emptied out all the little shampoo bottles to make it a bubble bath.

Then I carried her into the bathroom — tested the water to make sure it wasn't too hot — and when I lowered her in, she moaned with pleasure. "I'm in heaven," she said.

It hurt my leg, but I knelt on the floor next to the tub and with a wash-cloth I began to scrub her back, and as I bathed her, Ines wasn't the only one in heaven. It felt so good to care for someone — *to care for Ines* — and I felt flooded with love like a narcotic. It was the happiest I had been in years, and I scrubbed her all over, even her stumps, overcoming my fear.

I refreshed the bathwater several times, letting some of the dirty water out and bringing in new warm water — I didn't want this to end — and then I scrubbed her stubbly gray hair with my fingers, giving her a shampoo and scalp massage, and I kissed the back of her neck.

"I've missed you," I said.

"I've always loved you," she said, and a fantasy bloomed in my mind like a fever dream: I would take her back with me to LA and care for her like this all the time. What could be a better use of my life? I'd have Ines and George, my own strange family.

6.

EVENTUALLY, I GOT HER out of the tub, put her on the large marble counter by the sink, and swaddled her in towels. Then she took some of my toothpaste and cleaned her mouth with her finger.

After that, I carried her into the room and tucked her into the bed. I propped her half sitting up against the headboard, with pillows behind her, and pulled the blankets all the way up to her chin. Then she shed the towels and groaned with pleasure, feeling the cool sheets against her warm skin.

Getting clean seemed to have restored some of her dignity and she was more herself; she was still merry, but there was a greater lucidity in her eyes.

I took one of my T-shirts out of my bag. "Want to wear this, like pajamas?"

She nodded and slipped it over her head, and I checked my phone: no missed calls or messages from Mary.

Then I brought Ines a glass of water — I didn't want her to get dehydrated after a hot bath — and while she drank, I sat close to her on the edge of the bed, like she was my foundling, my patient. After finding her in that nasty tent, sleeping under a bridge, surrounded by garbage, I just wanted to comfort her. When she finished drinking, I took the glass from her, put it on the bedside table. "You ready to eat now?"

"Yes."

I found a Chinese restaurant on my phone and placed our order. They said they would deliver in forty-five minutes, and I put the phone back in my pocket and felt frustrated that there was still no word from Mary. She usually responded immediately when I texted my report each day, and I was eager to connect her with Ines. I said, "I haven't heard from your daughter yet, but she's going to be happy to talk to you when she does call."

"Maybe. She wasn't that friendly when we spoke, and we only talked a few times. But I understand. How could she ever forgive me?"

"Why *did* you get in touch with her after so many years?"

"I needed her address so that she can get my money someday. Her and Tracy. Tracy is the one you met. She saved me when I was dying from the gangrene, but even before that I put her in my will. And Mary."

"What money are you talking about, Ines?"

"I made peace with my mother last year. If you could call it that. I still had my legs then and I took the bus to Seattle, but she was disgusted by me, said I was a disgrace. But since my brothers were dead, she said she would put me in her will. No money now, of course, while she's alive because I'm a junkie. Which I understand. And I'm just like her, anyway. A terrible mother."

I regretted not saying something sooner, but I came out with it now. I said, "Ines, I was going to tell you later. Maybe tomorrow. I wanted you to settle in. But your mother died a few weeks ago. On Christmas."

She looked at me severely. "How do you know?"

"I looked it up."

"You're sure?"

"Yes. I'm sure. I read her death notice."

She nodded, believing me. "I had a feeling," she said. "A shadow feeling."

Then she began to cry gently. I took her hand, and she said, "I didn't think I'd be sad."

Then she rested her head on my shoulder, and I put my arms around her. It felt good to hold her, and after a while, she laughed quietly to herself, then pulled away from me and said, "I really am a homeless orphan now."

"That might not be such a bad thing. Did your mother tell you how much money she had?"

"Yeah. A lot. Millions, at least twenty-five million, maybe more. But I never thought it would happen. I figured I'd die long before she did."

"So do you realize what this means?"

Fear crossed her face, and she looked away from me. Then she said, "I only know one way to live now."

"With twenty-five million you can learn new things."

She let that sink in. "That *is* a lot of money. Maybe I could get special legs."

"That's right," I said, and then she laughed, back to her merry self. Methadone: the twenty-four-hour martini. And I could see that she didn't fully grasp how her life was going to change; it was too much information at once — her mother dead, the inheritance. So it didn't seem real. And it didn't seem real to me, either. On top of that I had an icy feeling in my stomach, thinking about Mary. She hadn't said anything about her mother getting in touch with her about a will.

I said, "Where is this lawyer you mentioned?"

"Seattle. I have his card in my backpack, but I haven't called him in a while. He wanted me to check in once a month, but I lost my phone when I got sick."

"But you told Mary, when you got in touch with her, that someday you might be getting money from your mother? A lot of money, and that your mother was in Seattle?"

"Yes."

"And when you asked for it, what address did Mary give you? Where did she say she lived?"

"I don't remember, but it was a boat. She said she lived on a boat in Marina del Rey. It sounded beautiful. That was the address she gave me and the lawyer."

"You put her in touch with the lawyer?"

"Yes. So she could email him her information. He wrote up my will as a favor to my mother."

"And Mary said she lived on a boat with her husband?"

"She didn't say anything about a husband. Said she lived with her boyfriend. Did she get married?"

"I think so. I met the husband."

"Nice man?"

"I only met him once," I said, and I felt sick thinking about Mary in my office a week ago. She had put on some kind of act, and I had fallen for it. She hadn't said a word about a will or being in touch with a lawyer, and then at the Tower Bar, when I asked her, she claimed not to know anything about her grandmother.

So that lie must have been to cover the real reason why she wanted me to find Ines: she wanted to be able to keep tabs on her, keep tabs on the twenty-five million.

But why the charade? Why lie to me about the grandmother? She wanted to act like her intentions were pure? That money wasn't part of this?

But I shouldn't have been surprised: clients almost always lie; there's always something they're ashamed of, something they want to hide. So what was Mary hiding? That she cared about money? I figured it had to be more than that, but what? And who the hell was Marrow?

But then I thought, *I don't care if she lied to me and if she and Marrow are playing games. It got me up here and I'm with Ines and that's all that matters.*

7.

Ines was delighted with the Chinese food and ate heartily.

There was a circular table near the entrance to the room, with a lamp and brochures, which I had cleared off, and that was our makeshift dining room table.

I even dimmed the lights, to make it feel like a restaurant, and I enjoyed watching her eat, as if it was my accomplishment: Doll the great provider.

Enjoying being together, I think we both put the thought of the inheritance out of our minds, it was too unfathomable, though before the food arrived, I had called the lawyer—the name on the card was Richard Koehler—and left a message on his office voice mail. I wasn't expecting to hear back from him on a Friday night, but maybe he'd call the next day.

When we finished eating, Ines wanted to smoke a cigarette.

So I bundled her up in my jacket and the blanket from my bed and rolled her out the side entrance. It was still snowing, and the parking lot was covered with a purifying white layer, and Ines cupped her cigarette like a hobo and seemed to take enormous pleasure in it. Then I checked my phone: it was nearly nine and there was still no response from Mary.

When Ines finished her cigarette, she needed to use the bathroom.

I rolled her back to the room, and when I lifted her onto the toilet seat, she gripped the sides to steady herself, and I said, "How have you been doing this since your operation?"

Soon as the words came out of my mouth, I realized it was a dumb question, but she answered patiently, "At the bridge, I just drag myself down by the water. That's where everybody goes."

I nodded and went to leave the room. I said, "Call out when you're done."

"You can stay, I'm just peeing."

So I stayed, listened to her pass her water, then carried her to bed, like a child. I tucked her in, sat on the edge, and told her I was going to go to the ER, to get my leg checked and get some antibiotics. I said, "Part of the reason this scar on my face is so bad is that it got infected."

"It suits you," she said. Then she raised up, kissed me on the cheek, right on the scar, then lay back down.

"You're too kind," I said, smiling, and got up to leave.

But she lifted her hand to stop me and said, "Hold me a little while? I know I don't look so good, but with the lights off, we can pretend that I'm like I used to be."

I said, "We don't have to pretend anything, Ines."

Then I turned off the light and removed my boots. I lay on top of the covers, behind her, and pulled her close. I hadn't been like this with anyone in five years. I closed my eyes and kissed her neck, gently. She smelled clean from the bath. We lay like that for a while, and I listened to her breathing.

Then she said, "I always had such big eyes for you."

She pushed herself closer to me then and I felt the fever dream coming back: a desire to spend the rest of my life loving her, caring for her.

Then her breaths started growing faint, and half asleep, she said, "I love you, Happy."

I went to say it back, but then I hesitated, suddenly very scared that those words might be a promise I couldn't keep, after all.

So I said nothing and we lay there in silence.

Then after a while, I thought, *Don't be a coward,* and I whispered, "I love you, Ines."

But she didn't say anything back, and I realized she was asleep and hadn't heard what I'd said.

8.

ABOUT TWO INCHES OF SNOW had fallen, which was not enough to keep me from driving to the hospital. I let the car warm up a second and put on the radio. It was Stevie Nicks again. It felt like I hadn't heard Fleetwood Mac in a long time and now twice in one day. This time she was singing: "Now you're keeping some demon down, stop draggin' my, stop draggin' my, stop draggin' my heart around." Then Mary called, *finally*. I answered: "Hello, Mary."

Except it wasn't Mary. "It's Hoyt. I'm using Mary's phone."

"She got my message? She knows I found her mother?"

"Yes, but she's very sick. Has a terrible flu or something. She just woke up and saw your message but is too weak to call. She asked me to. But she'll speak to her mother tomorrow."

"All right."

"And we'll fly up Sunday. If Mary's feeling better. You have the mother in the hotel?"

"Yes."

"Okay. Good. I'll have Leland get you a flight out tomorrow afternoon."

"That's not going to work. I need to stay with Ines, at least until Mary gets here."

"Why?"

"Because she needs help. She's had both her legs amputated above the knee."

"*What?* Why?"

"She got frostbite and gangrene."

"When did this happen?"

"She must have gone into the hospital sometime in November, which is when Mary stopped hearing from her. She was let out a few weeks ago."

"All right, you stay there until we get there. Where are you right now? I hear music."

I turned the car radio off. "I'm in the car. I'm on my way to the hospital."

"Something else is wrong with the mother?"

"No, she's in the room sleeping. I had an accident and cut my leg and need to get some stitches."

"The mother's alone? She doesn't need you?"

"She can be alone for a few hours. I need to get this leg looked at."

"How did you hurt yourself?"

"I fell. Listen, I want to ask you: why didn't you or Mary say anything to me about being in touch with Ines's lawyer? If nothing else, he might have known how we could find her. That was an important piece of information."

Marrow was silent. Then in a measured way, he said, "You were hired to find this woman, Mr. Doll. That's it. Got it? I've paid you very nicely. Much more than your regular fee."

"Mary should have told me about the lawyer, and I'd still like to know your real name."

He was silent, then hung up the phone.

9.

THE ER DOCTOR WHO took care of me at the hospital was a nice man, a redhead in his midforties, with twinkly eyes and chubby pink hands. But those chubby hands were not to be underestimated — this redheaded doctor was talented with the thread and needle; his hands were dexterous and sure.

I watched him stitching up my leg, his face intent with care and professionalism, and I thought how there's more good people in the world than bad, but that bit of news never seems to make the front page.

After the doctor finished closing my wounds, the ER nurses wanted me to rest a moment before leaving, and I lay back on the small bed, private behind my blue curtains, and I thought about Ines waiting for me back in the hotel. It was nuts but thinking of her I could literally feel my heart expand with tenderness and a near bursting sensation, like something out of a bad poem. But to hell with that. It felt good!

But then I caught myself. I had been down this road with her before: this impossible and deluded wish to save someone who could not be saved. And, of course, the Buddhists have a name for doing that sort of thing: samsara. Cyclical suffering. I had been reading all about it.

And, under another name, I had already been learning about it for years in my analysis. What the Buddhists called samsara, Freud called "repetition compulsion." I'd had plenty of both.

And to make things worse, it wasn't just the Buddha and Freud who had weighed in on this, there was Einstein, too, with his definition of insanity: "Doing the same thing over and over again and expecting different results."

That was certainly a heady trio to defy, which gave me pause, but then I swung my legs off the hospital bed, suddenly feeling cocky. I told myself I had changed. I was different from the me of thirteen years ago. I could take on Einstein, Freud, and the Buddha. After all, I had love on my side. That had to be worth something.

10.

IT HAD STOPPED SNOWING and was around 12:30 when I got back to the hotel with twenty stitches, a bottle of antibiotics, and directions not to get my leg wet for the next ten days.

I used the side entrance off the parking lot, and when I went in the room, something felt different. I must have picked up a smell that my ancient brain knew the meaning of but not my modern brain. Then I turned on the light and Ines was lying on the bed with the covers pulled back. A rig was in her arm, her head was slumped to the side, and she was dead. A spoon and lighter and a small baggie were on the bedside table. She had died with her eyes open, and I dug my fingers into her blue-tinged neck: no throb, no pulse.

Frantic, I put my head to her chest and listened for the hammer. Didn't hear it. Then I tried CPR and gave her mouth to mouth.

It was the first time I had kissed her in thirteen years and the last time.

I stepped back from the bed and looked at her.

Her light green eyes were almost white in death, and her amputated body, like a ragged garment, had been discarded, left behind, no longer needed.

Hysterical and numb, I went to the closet.

Her backpack was still up on the shelf. She couldn't have reached it. But her jacket was hanging up: if she had the rig in her pockets, maybe she could have gotten to it.

But then I looked at her wheelchair: it was still in the corner where I had left it, with the blanket still on it from when we had gone outside for her to smoke.

Which meant she hadn't gotten out of bed and rolled herself to the closet. Which meant she didn't bring the junk with her. Which meant it was brought *to* her. And who would do that? Who would have the heroin? *Scruggs. It must have been Scruggs.*

He must have beaten Tracy and the other girl Ines had spoken to. They told him we were at La Quinta, and they gave him my name. Then the front desk gave him my room number. It was easy enough to get that information.

So Scruggs had come and broken into the room and murdered Ines. *He said he would kill her, and he did.*

I could see him standing over her, putting the needle into her arm.

And he had come with the other two. To help deal with me and give me payback.

And then I thought, *But I wasn't here. Wasn't here to defend her. And now she's dead. Because of me.*

Then for what seemed like a long time, I just stood there. Might have been one of those catatonic trances. Where you have a foot in both worlds, unsure where to be.

Then I picked up the phone and made the call.

11.

FIRST THE COPS CAME and then the paramedics.

The two cops were young and big. Early thirties, beefy, with their heavy winter coats thrown open. One had ruddy cheeks, one had onion breath. One was Hawkins, one was Novik.

They didn't love my story, but, in the end, they bought it, maybe because it was true: I wasn't in the room when Ines OD'd, and I wasn't doing drugs with her. I was a retired LA cop who had been hired to find Ines, a homeless woman, and while I was at the hospital, getting stitches in my leg, she OD'd.

I showed them the plastic bracelet from the hospital, which had a time stamp, and I also told them that my leg wounds had come from three men at a camp under the Fourth Avenue Bridge, where I had found Ines. I said, "They were beating an old man, and I stepped in to break it up. I had a heavy Maglite that I used as a baton, and that's when I got stabbed."

That didn't seem to impress them, and they searched the room for more drugs, looking for something to bust me with, but, of course, they didn't find anything. After they finished searching the room, they had a private confab, and I watched the paramedics fuss with Ines.

Then Hawkins and his ruddy cheeks left the room, and Novik and his onion breath came over to me, and he said they weren't going to bring me in. "We believe you weren't here when she died."

"Good. Because what you need to do is go over to that camp and get ahold of this guy Scruggs." I had been waiting for the right moment and this was it. "He's a dealer, deals to all the homeless junkies, and he said he was going to kill Ines when I took her out of there. He didn't like me interfering with the old man they were beating up, and I hit him hard with my Maglite. More than once. And so he took it out on her."

I pointed at Ines and the cop looked over. The paramedics were getting ready to lift her onto the gurney. "My point is she didn't have any drugs when she came here. So this guy Scruggs must have showed up while I was in the hospital, and killed her."

Novik looked at Ines — a double amputee, her arms covered in tracks — and I knew what he was thinking: *She's just a junkie.*

He said, "How do you know she didn't stash it somewhere. Junkies are tricky that way."

"Look at her. She couldn't move. She was in bed. She didn't have it with her."

"Maybe she called a friend, had it delivered. You were out of the room."

"She didn't have a cell phone."

"There's a room phone."

Fuck.

I looked at him and then went to the phone, spoke to the front desk. "Can you check if any calls were made from this room tonight? It's important. It's part of the investigation."

Novik looked at me. He didn't like me using the word *investigation.* The desk clerk said, "No calls out or in tonight." I held the phone out to Novik. "Want to speak to him? He says, no calls."

"Hang up."

I hung up the phone. Hawkins came back into the room. Novik said to me, "How would this guy Scruggs know where you took her?"

Hawkins interrupted: "What are you talking about?"

Novik gestured at me. "He thinks some dealer came here and OD'd her on purpose." Hawkins frowned and shrugged, like this was funny *and* ridiculous, and Novik asked me again, "So how would he know where to find you? You told him, after you beat him up, come to La Quinta?"

"No, she told a friend, a young girl, where we were going, and he must have beaten the information out of her."

"You're crazy," Novik said. "Most likely the friend came by looking for a warm room and a party. You know how many junkies OD every night in the motels around here? More than babies are born at the hospital."

"That's not how it happened," I said, feeling like I might start to lose it. "She wouldn't have shot up. She was *forced* to. You should treat this like a homicide. She was on methadone. She would know that she would overdose."

Both cops laughed at me. Hawkins said, "Junkies OD from methadone and shooting up all the time. They love it. They drink the street methadone like it's beer, and then they shoot up."

I shook my head. "She wouldn't have shot up. She was forced." What I didn't say, but what I was screaming inside was: *She wouldn't do that to me! Not tonight!*

But doubt began to creep in. Maybe she *had* stashed it somewhere or maybe Tracy had come by to party, and when Ines OD'd, Tracy had fled. But then I said to the cops, "Let's go to the front desk and check the security cameras. This guy Scruggs came here and killed her."

"Drop it," said Novik, and he was getting impatient.

"I'm telling you this is a homicide," I said. "Let's go look at the lock."

I went to the door, and they didn't follow me. I studied the lock: there were some scratches on it but nothing significant. But that didn't matter: the magnetic locks on hotel doors were shit, like having no lock at all. I went back into the room.

Novik said, "Nothing, right?"

"That lock is crap, a million ways to get in." Then I grabbed his arm. "I'm telling you she was killed. Let's go to the front desk. See the security footage."

He yanked his arm back. I was crazy to touch a cop. "Don't fucking touch me!"

Novik then pushed me down onto the bed, shouted at me, "You want us to bring you in? Is that what you fucking want? Or are you going to get ahold of yourself?"

I looked at them. They weren't going to help me, and I definitely didn't want to be brought in. Because now I had things to do. On my own.

I said, playing calm, "I'm sorry. I overreacted."

The cops looked at me, then Hawkins said, "You going to contact the family or should we? You said you're working for the daughter, right?"

"I'll call her tomorrow. It's the middle of the night."

The cops nodded their agreement, then the paramedics started to roll Ines out: she was covered with a sheet. I stood up fast. "Wait!"

They stopped rolling her. I went over by her side. I could feel Novik and Hawkins staring at me. I pulled back the sheet and looked at her face. They hadn't closed her eyes, and she looked right through me.

Then I sat back down on the bed and waited for them all to leave.

12.

It was nearly 2:30 in the morning, and nobody was at the front desk.

I hit the little bell, and a young, balding man emerged from the back office. His nameplate said Halladay, and he had bad posture, bad dandruff, and bad teeth. He was in his late twenties, but he'd been working the night shift all his life. I had spoken to him twice: once for him to call 911 and once to prove my point to Novik. I'd also seen him poke his nervous head in my room and then disappear when the paramedics first arrived.

I said, "I'm Mr. Doll from 114. Thanks for your help tonight." I was keeping myself nice and contained, presenting a sane front, but I didn't feel sane. I could feel twitches moving under the skin of my face like bedbugs, but I kept them in. It was important to keep everything in. To save my energy, to load myself like a bullet. *Ines was dead.*

"I'm very sorry about your friend," said Halladay.

"Me, too." Then I described Tracy, indicated that she was homeless, and asked if she had come through the lobby or if he had seen her anywhere around the hotel.

"No, nobody like that, no homeless people."

"What about a skinhead guy, then, with face tats. Maybe with two other rough-looking skinheads. Seen anybody like that tonight?"

"Nobody like that. Why are you asking about these people?" I was making him nervous. A person had died in my room that night, and he kept looking at my scar.

I said, "I think one of those people OD'd my friend. Does your security camera cover the side door?"

"No. Just the front of the parking lot and the lobby."

"I'd like to look at the footage."

"I can't do that."

"Why not?"

"I just can't. You can speak to my manager in the morning."

Staying sane, staying cool, I put a hundred-dollar bill on the counter. "Let's go look at the security footage. If the camera covers the front of the lot, could you see somebody walking to the side door?"

He didn't touch the hundred-dollar bill. He said, "I can't do that, Mr. Doll. I'd like you to go back to your room."

Then he looked to his right, nervously, unconsciously: we were being filmed right now, which maybe explained his hesitancy to take my bribe and allow me into his back office. So I pocketed the money for the sake of the camera and his paranoia, and said, "Check the footage yourself, tell me what you see, and I'll give you five hundred dollars."

"I can't do that."

"Five hundred dollars."

"It's not worth my job."

"You won't lose your job."

"Please go back to your room."

He was cowardly yet brave, and he was pissing me off. *Ines was dead!* I snarled, "Just do it!"

"You need to —"

Before he could finish, I slammed my hand down on the counter between us, and he shrank back, frightened. I was losing my containment, and I thought of coming over the counter, and he saw it in my eyes.

"I need you to leave the lobby, sir. I don't want to have to call the police." He then actually made the movie gesture of lifting the receiver of his desk phone, and I wanted to smack him, but then I thought, *Fuck it. I don't need to see the security footage. I know what happened.*

And I reloaded myself, put the bullet back in the chamber. For the right target.

I left Halladay and limped back to my room.

I put on my coat, grabbed the Maglite, and headed out to the parking lot. I felt like I might need more than one weapon and in the trunk of the car was a tire iron.

13.

THE SLOPE DOWN TO the junkyard was covered in snow, and I nearly slipped. The lamps on the bridge above had been turned off for the night, it was very dark, and under the bridge, only a single fire still burned: one of the barrels emitted jagged flashes of orange light and plenty of smoke. Somebody must have been tending to the fire recently — it was full of flaming wooden boards — but no one was about. They were all huddled in their tents, holding on for another night. I stepped by the fire and shouted, "SCRUGGS COME OUT HERE!"

In my left hand I held the Maglite and in my right was the tire iron.

"SCRUGGS!"

My heart was pounding. I felt like I was flooring my car and driving straight for a wall. Then I hit the wall and what I had been containing, like a strait-jacket, was now out, and I suddenly knew I had come here to die, to not let Ines get too much of a head start, and with this realization there was a return to sanity, and I must have blacked out for a moment, gone completely inward, because then suddenly there were about twenty of them surrounding me, and I stepped back to the perimeter, to the edge of the light, so that nobody could get behind me.

A little too late, I didn't want to die.

Scruggs and the other two sick boys emerged from the darkness behind the fire, stepped through the line of people, and a very large man, also with a shaved head, joined them. He had a brown army blanket around his shoulders, like a cape, and he was round and solid, like a wrecking ball. He was five nine, 300 pounds, and had no neck. He had the bearing of a beggar king, and he wasn't yet thirty. This must be the Fat Man Ines had spoken about. His eyes were like black diamonds. Scruggs shouted at me, "YOU'RE FUCKED, COMING BACK HERE!"

I was no longer insane, but I had a role to play. I shouted, "YOU KILLED INES!"

"FUCK YOU!"

Then somebody in the crowd threw a piece of burning wood at me and it jackknifed through the cold air, shedding sparks like a comet, mesmerizing me as it sailed past, and then too late out of the corner of my eye, I saw a dervish of a man swinging what looked like a baseball bat right into my one kidney, and an explosive sick feeling jolted through my whole body, and I fell to the ground, but out of the torque of that pain, I backhanded the man with the tire iron, heard the crack of metal on skull, and then I swiped at someone's legs to my left with the Maglite, blasting a knee, and then Scruggs and the sick boys and a handful of others were closing in on me, like jackals in the firelight, and I managed to stand, swinging my two weapons wildly, to keep them at bay, and behind them, like a general, was the Fat Man, and then I was hit in the face with a flaming board, and the black sky wheeled above me, gashed down the middle with fire, and then there was a plunge, an endless fall into a darkness without sound.

14.

I DREAMT THAT I was being stomped by a terrifying giant, a primordial man the size of a tree. And I knew him. It was the giant from the recurring nightmare I'd had as a child. Every night, I'd dream I was alone in our little front yard, unable to move or run, and I could hear a giant's pounding footsteps climbing the hill to my house, on his way to find me, and then kill me.

But each night, he never arrived. He only threatened for years. I never saw him once. Which was perhaps worse. There was no satisfaction, even in the negative, because underneath the terror was a wish for him to get it over with already, to show himself and to wipe me out. The fear was too much to bear.

Then the dream of the giant stopped for decades, though I never stopped waiting for him, and now, finally, he had revealed himself and he was as cruel as I had always imagined.

He was stomping me to death because he hated me, thought I was disgusting, and I was covering up like a little animal, trying not to die, but half wishing for it, too, as I had as a boy, and then I heard a deep voice: "Don't mark his face too much! And try not to break his ribs!"

The voice woke me from my dream, and I looked up and in the glow of the fire, there was the Fat Man, and around me, stomping me, kicking me, were the sick boys.

Then the Fat Man said, "That's enough," and the blows stopped right away, with unexpected discipline, and I couldn't move. Had I been stomped into paralysis? No, not entirely because I could feel that the stitches in my leg had been kicked open. Scruggs said, "Let me cut his throat."

"Don't be an idiot," said the Fat Man. "Lift him up. Let me have a taste."

Scruggs and the other tall sick boy hoisted me up by the armpits and stood me in front of their boss. But they had to hold on to me — I had the legs of a puppet — and all around us were the members of the camp, and I saw Tracy and Samuel, the old Black man, standing next to each other, staring at me, and then the Fat Man backhanded me across the face, with all three hundred pounds behind it, and the force of the blow was so great, the two skinheads couldn't help but drop me, and my head bounced off the Fat Man's boot.

Then I blacked out for a second, and when I came back, the Fat Man was lifting my head with the toe of his boot, like he was inspecting me, and then he let my head drop back to the ground, hard, and I looked up at him, like an ant to a giant. Some dreams do come true.

Then he lifted his black boot into the air, held it over my head. He smiled at me then, and I saw his teeth had been filed to points, like sharks' teeth.

"DO IT!" somebody shouted, and he lifted his boot higher, to make the blow more devastating, and then his boot came rushing down — he was going to crush my skull with his enormous weight — and I turned away, but at the last moment, he slowed up completely and just lightly tapped my face with the sole of his shoe, and my body convulsed involuntarily, like he had sparked me with electricity, and they all laughed, the Fat Man the loudest. And his sharp teeth glinted in the firelight. He had probably done that to himself in prison. I'd seen dental work like that before. Gave an inmate one more way to survive.

When he finished laughing, he shouted, "Sit him up!"

Scruggs and the tall one sat me up, one on each side, and the big man squatted down in front of me and removed from his back pocket a pint of Jack Daniel's. "Pinch his nose closed," he ordered. His charnel breath, in my face, was hot and rancid, and Scruggs clamped down on my nose, and *he* looked like a hell fiend: the tattooed skulls were alive on his face, twitching with excitement, and his eyes were filled with murder lust. I had to open my mouth to breathe, and then the Fat Man, with one massive hand under my jaw tilted my head back, and with his other hand he shoved the bottle of Jack into my mouth, pouring whisky down my throat.

I thrashed spastically, dislodging the bottle, but that only made them more determined, and the two sick boys tightened their hold on me, and the Fat Man forced the bottle into my mouth again, like I was a nursing babe. Then it was either swallow the whisky or be drowned by it, and when the bottle was empty, he let me flop to the ground.

I was blinded by the alcohol, but I could feel them rifling through my pockets and grabbing at me, and the Fat Man said, "See, now he'll just be another drunk floater, but if you cut his neck then we'd have problems," and Scruggs said, "I want his jacket," and someone else said, "I want his boots," but the Fat Man said, "A floater might lose his jacket but probably not his boots," and then I heard nothing else.

15.

WHEN THEY THREW ME into the lake, consciousness returned like a plate of glass shattering, and I screamed and my mouth was filled with freezing black water, and Scruggs, using a wooden board, pushed me out deeper. He and the Fat Man and the others stood at the edge of the bank, beneath the bridge, watching, and my wet clothes clung to me like cement.

I began to sink, then broke the surface, and then almost immediately went back under. Where they had tossed me in was where the river fed into the lake, pouring over a dam, creating a strong current, which pulled me down and dragged me to the south, away from the bridge.

I managed to break the surface again and gulp some air.

But my arms were too heavy and the freezing black water pulled me down again, worse than any nightmare of drowning, and I was nearly ready to quit, I was down there a long time, being pushed along, always deeper, but then I screamed *No!* in my mind and fought my way back up, and when I emerged, I was no longer under the bridge, and I couldn't see my attackers, and they couldn't see me. I was moving parallel to the snow-covered bank at the bottom of the slope, which was about twenty yards away, but felt like a mile.

I had this instinct then to fool the water, to pretend not to fight, like going still for a bear in the woods, and it seemed to work. I rolled onto my back and the water allowed me to float along, and I was going farther and farther downstream from the bridge, just looking at the winter sky, and I suddenly felt peaceful: I had drunk a whole pint of whisky and my body was beginning to shut down. I thought I might even try to go to sleep, the water wasn't cold anymore, and then I thought, *Just try a little swimming, try to get to the edge and go to sleep on the snow,* and then I had this happy idea that not only had I fooled the water but also the Fat Man, because I said to myself, *You can't kill a drunk, everybody knows that,* and all relaxed now, feeling that I was protected, I swam for the snowy bank, lifting my sodden arms, but doing so very slowly so as not to rouse the lake and make it angry, and the lake, I could tell, was lulled by my cunning and continued to think that all in good time it was going to consume me and bring an end to my pain, but I was a stronger swimmer than it realized, and there was this as well: Scruggs had probably saved my life by stealing my heavy coat.

16.

I WOKE UP AROUND NOON in Samuel's tent. He was sitting cross-legged, right next to me, and I was lying naked in a sleeping bag. Some dim light came through the skin of the tent, and there was just enough room for the two of us. I knew immediately where I was: on some level I must have known for hours. He saw that I was awake and said, "How are you feeling?"

"Not good," I said, and I had lost most of my voice. I was also burning up, had a bad fever headache, and my leg throbbed. I unzipped the sleeping bag and saw that he had bound my thigh with rags. So much for keeping the stitches dry, or even sewn up for that matter. I indicated the leg. "Thank you."

"Can you sit up a little, drink something?"

I managed to get to one elbow, my body was sore and covered in purple and green bruises from being kicked and stomped, and he handed me a crinkled old plastic water bottle that he must have filled somewhere in town. I sipped a little, and then he gave me two antibiotic pills and two Tylenol, telling me what everything was and that I should take it all. "You might have pneumonia," he said. Then he gestured to the pills he had put in my hand. "This is all from Tracy. From when *she* had pneumonia."

I'll do whatever this man tells me, I thought, and I managed to get the pills down and some more water, then I collapsed back to the floor. "How did I get here?"

He told me that he and Tracy had snuck out of the camp, maybe twenty minutes after I was thrown into the lake, and that they had found me about a hundred yards south of the bridge, lying on the bank in the snow. After that, they had managed, before I died of exposure, to drag me back to the camp, and I had even walked most of the way, which I had no memory of.

"Thank you for saving me," I said in a hoarse whisper.

"I'd call an ambulance, but I don't have a phone and Tracy doesn't have one. If we ask anyone else, they might tell the sick boys — everybody wants to be on their good side — and you won't survive another beating. They don't know you're alive."

"That's good," I rasped, then a bad shiver went through me, and my head was killing me.

He saw me shudder. "You all right?"

"I'm in a lot of pain."

"We can take care of that," he said, and handed me another crinkly plastic water bottle. This one was a quarter filled with a red liquid that looked like cough syrup.

"What's this? Codeine?"

"Methadone. It'll help you sleep. Help your body heal. Then when you're strong enough, I'll sneak you outta here. I used to be a physician's assistant, I know what I'm talking about."

"Okay," I said, and got back up on my elbow. I thought again, *I'll do whatever this man tells me,* and I drank the sweet-tasting red methadone.

I handed the empty bottle back to him and said, "They killed Ines."

"She was a beautiful person," he said.

Then I closed my eyes and when I woke up next it was two o'clock in the morning. I had slept for almost fourteen hours.

17.

AROUND THREE A.M., with just one fire burning, Samuel led the way, and we circled the quiet, dark camp, and on the other side of the bridge from where I had entered both times, we took a different, less visible path to the road, and nobody saw us.

I was in my stiff, damp clothing, with a blue plastic tarp around my shoulders, and I had to drag my injured leg.

And my whole body was sore, covered in welts and bruises, but before we had set out, Samuel had made me a meal to give me strength and courage: a can of Campbell's chicken soup, which he heated up on a little Sterno, a hamburger bun with warm Crisco oil smeared on it, and a cowboy coffee also prepared on the Sterno. It was all absurdly delicious — I hadn't any food in more than twenty-four hours — and then, a veritable pharmacy unto himself, Samuel had provided me with two more Tylenol, one more antibiotic, and a smaller dose of the sweet-tasting methadone as a nightcap.

So, considering everything, I wasn't doing too bad, thanks to his nursing, and when we climbed over the guardrail and got to the road, I saw that my rental car was gone. But it didn't really matter: the car would have been useless to me; the sick boys had taken my keys. Either they had boosted the car, or it had been towed away. They had also relieved me of my wallet and my phone.

Samuel said, "Cross the bridge and then after a few blocks, there's a gas station with a pay phone, which I think works, and you can call 911, go to the hospital and get your leg looked at."

"I might try to make it back to my hotel, I've got some extra cash in my suitcase. Then I'll go to the hospital." My voice was still raspy as hell, but, amazingly, I didn't feel feverish or have a sore throat, which might have been the methadone working its magic.

"How far is it to your hotel?"

"Maybe ten miles."

"That's crazy."

"I know. I just don't want to have to answer a lot of questions if I call 911 and the cops show up. But I'll figure it out. I'm just gonna start walking." I wasn't thinking so straight, but I just really didn't want to call the police.

"I understand," he said, and there was nothing more he could do for me: he had no money to lend and no phone to call a cab. We shook hands and I said, "I'm gonna pay you back real soon."

"This was *me* paying *you* back," he said. "We're even."

I didn't want to fight him on it, it was a point of pride, and then he smiled and had one more gift for me. He handed me a joint — half tobacco, half weed — and lit it for me. "For your walk."

Then he scrambled down the hill, and I started limping my way back to the hotel, smoking the joint. I went to cross the bridge, but then had another idea, a real good one, and I kept going straight.

I limped two miles south on the Deschutes Parkway, half floating on the methadone and the weed, until I found the old green van. I had given the saddle soap man one hundred bucks: maybe he'd drive me to La Quinta. I knocked on the back door. Waited. Knocked again. The van shifted and the old man called out, "Go away!"

I said, loudly, "I'm the guy who gave you a hundred bucks. I need help."

There was silence and then the van doors swung open, and a flashlight burned my eyes. Then the light was lowered to my chest and when my eyes adjusted, I was looking into the black hole at the end of a rifle barrel.

I dropped the blue tarp and lifted my hands in surrender, and the old man, sitting up on his mattress, was holding his rifle one-handed, like Chuck Connors in *The Rifleman,* and in his other paw was the flashlight. He'd been sleeping with his leather trooper's hat on, with the ear flaps down, to stay warm, but he was awake now. "What the fuck you want?" he growled. "I'll blow a hole through you."

I raised my hands even higher and said, "I'm the guy who was looking for the woman. I showed you her picture. You told me where she was. I gave you a hundred bucks."

The light went back up to my face and then lowered back down. "Oh, yeah, I remember you. That's a memorable scar you have. What the hell happened?"

On the way to the hotel, I told him.

18.

HALLADAY WAS AT THE front desk again. When he saw me, it looked like his knees buckled. I had ditched the blue tarp in the dumpster outside, but I still looked like hell. I said, "I was mugged. I need a new key."

"Are you all right, Mr. Doll?"

"I'm fine. Just want to get into my room." My voice was raspy from the hypothermia, but my throat still didn't hurt, and while Halladay made the key, I thought about the old man's rifle. I was going to need something like that when I returned to the bridge. But first I had to get my strength back.

I also had to contact Mary, let her know her mother was dead.

Halladay gave me the new key, and I said, "Do you have a computer for guests to check their email?"

"In the business center, on the second floor."

He pointed to the elevator I had never used. I thought of going up there to check my email and find Mary's phone number, but then I figured it could wait until the morning: I needed to get out of my damp, stiff clothes and go to the hospital.

"Thanks," I said, and limped to the room.

The switch on the wall didn't work, and so I walked a little farther into the darkness and felt for and then turned on the lamp, which was on the round table where Ines and I had eaten our Chinese food, and when the light came on, I looked up and saw that a man was standing against the far wall. He was pointing a silenced .22 at me, and he was tall, wearing a black baseball hat and black winter coat, and in his right hand was the long-barreled gun, and in his left hand was the TV remote, which he aimed at the flat-screen mounted on the wall.

Then the TV, tuned to ESPN, came on real loud to cover the sound he was about to make with his muffled .22 — he was playing things extra safe.

But that action with the remote gave me just a fraction of a second and on an impulse, I lifted up the thick circular table and charged at him with it in front of me, like a shield. As I did this, the lamp came unplugged and fell to the carpet, and there were two little thuds in the table. He'd had time to fire twice, and then I smashed into him, hard, and he crumpled to his knees and the gun fell from his hand. In the glow from the TV, he bent at the waist to get the .22, and I was still holding the table like a shield, and I chopped the back of his head with the table edge, knocking him flat to the ground. But not hard enough, because he crawled on his knees for the .22, fighting for his life and wanting to take mine, and he got the .22 in his hand, but before he could spin about and shoot me, I brought the table down hard on the crown of his head, and he went face-first to the carpet. Then, in a spasm of violence and fear, I brought the table edge down two more times, and when I stopped, I saw with horror what I had done. Then I threw the table to the side, and slid to the floor myself, and sat there with my back against the bed.

I stared straight ahead, breathing rapidly, then looked over at the dead man. I had knocked off his black baseball cap, and I saw that he had silver-blonde hair, streaked now with blood. The blonde hair looked familiar, but I didn't know why. Then the room phone rang. I crawled over to it between the two beds. It was Halladay. I figured he was going to tell me that the police were on their way, that shots had been heard. He said, "There's been a complaint about the TV, Mr. Doll."

"Sorry," I said. "I'll take care of it." I hung up and turned off the TV and the room went dark. This gave me a moment to think. I wasn't ready for the cops. Not yet.

Then I turned a light on and checked the wallet of the dead man. His California driver's license said he was Leland Roscoe, which was the name of Hoyt Marrow's assistant.

And everything clicked into place.

PART III

1.

I WRAPPED THE dead man's head in a towel so that the carpet wouldn't get any more stained than it was. I had no intention now to call the police. Ines was dead, and *I* would be her wheel of justice.

But I wasn't in my right mind, and my excuse — if I was to give one — wouldn't be something like PTSD, it would be it's-happening-*RIGHT-NOW* stress disorder.

When I finished wrapping the dead man's head, I went back to his wallet: he had about five hundred dollars cash and a plastic room key for the Hampton Inn.

The key was in a paper sleeve, with the room number written on it, and I had driven past that Hampton Inn numerous times. It was about two miles down the road, and I wondered if Roscoe was working alone. Could there be someone waiting for him back at his room?

In his pockets were his cell phone, a set of house keys attached to a Mercedes car fob, a switchblade, and a little baggie of cocaine, which was a welcome find. I snorted two bumps for my pain, made a cup of coffee in the little coffee maker, and changed my clothes.

Then I put on the dead man's winter jacket, put the long-barreled .22 in the waistband of my pants, and went looking for a Mercedes, pressing the key fob like calling for a dog that's run away.

Three blocks from the hotel, the car flashed its lights at me in response, and I felt like it was happy to see me, though, of course, it was the other way around. Without ID, I couldn't fly back to LA, couldn't get my hands on Marrow, but I had a vehicle now: a low-slung, black, two-door SL550, with CA license plates and no rental car markings.

I slid behind the wheel and the insurance card in the glove compartment had an interesting name on it: Haze Langdon, the owner of the house on MacArthur Drive. Somewhere he factored into all this.

There was no back seat, and on the passenger seat there were a lot of paper bags from take-out places, which indicated two things: (1) Roscoe had been working solo — nobody could have sat in all that crap — and (2) he had been following me and staking me out for a few days.

I drove back to La Quinta, the Mercedes handled like a torpedo, and in the room, I washed out the bloodstain on the carpet as best I could, using a washcloth and shampoo. Then I made another cup of coffee and purposely spilled that on the carpet, covering one stain with another.

Surprising myself, I managed to unscrew the top of the circular table, which had two .22 slugs in it, and I threw that in the trunk of the Mercedes, along with all my stuff and Ines's belongings.

Then I parked the Mercedes right next to the side entrance and limped back to the room.

I got Roscoe into a sitting position, leaning him against the bed, and from the front he didn't look too bad. He was a handsome kid, almost pretty, and all the damage had been done to the back of his head. But his blue eyes were open and held a look of shocked betrayal, which was unnerving. So I put his baseball cap back on and tilted it so that he couldn't see me.

Then I took a deep breath, grabbed him under both arms, and when I lifted him up, I could feel the water-bloated wounds in my right leg break open as I got him to his feet. He was roughly my height, six two, and not easy to handle. He must have weighed about 200 pounds.

But I managed to get him out to the hall and pretended to drunk-walk him down to the exit, murmuring things like, "Buddy, you really shouldn't have had so much tequila" and "I hate it when you get this wasted."

And nobody came out of their room. It was nearly four a.m.

When I got him outside, I swept the crap off the passenger seat of the Mercedes and sat him down.

Still murmuring platitudes to an intoxicated friend and an invisible audience, I put the seat belt on him, which kept his body upright, though his head slumped forward. His driver's license had said he was twenty-eight years old. He was a young man but not anymore.

I got behind the wheel and parked the car in a dark corner of the lot. When I looked back, I could barely see him through the narrow windshield, and if someone did see him, I told myself, they'd just think he was a sleeping drunk. Or so I hoped. Also, it was late, and the risk was minimal. Nobody was around.

I limped across the frigid lot, and in the room, I did a final scan and cleanup. I pocketed the .22 shells and collected the bloody washcloth and towel and put them in a plastic La Quinta laundry bag. Then I left $140 for the maid, which was all the cash I'd had hidden in my bag, and I dragged myself down the hall to the lobby.

The only thing I had left in the room was Ines's wheelchair, which I hoped the hotel would give to charity, though leaving it behind was difficult, like I was leaving her behind. But I didn't have room for the chair. At some point, where nobody might see me, I had to get the dead man into the trunk.

I rang the bell on the counter, and Halladay emerged. I thought I would look less like a murderer if I checked out in person. Not sure why. Maybe it was instinct. Or maybe it was the coke I had snorted, or the weed I had smoked, or the methadone I had drunk. Whatever it was, I knew I wasn't quite sane anymore. Dangling from my hand was the plastic bag of bloody towels.

I gave Halladay my plastic room key, said I was checking out.

He was more relaxed now, glad to see me go. He said, "Everything all right, Mr. Doll?"

"Fine," I said.

"Keep the charges on your card or the card that made the reservation?"

That was a good question. I said, "The one that made the reservation. And which one was that? I forgot. My employer, right?" The dead man in the Mercedes, Roscoe, had made the reservation, and I was curious now what card he had used.

Halladay looked at his computer screen. "An Amex card. Haze Langdon. That's your employer?"

"Yes. He's a good man," I said, and I thought, *That bastard again.*

"Would you like a printout of your charges?"

"No, that's not necessary. Listen, I spilled some coffee in the room. Will Mr. Langdon get charged for that?"

"No, we don't usually charge for that. There are so many spills. Half the carpets are covered in coffee and all sorts of things."

"I can imagine," I said. Then I added, "I want to use the business center computer. Do I need a key or anything?"

"No, the center's not locked."

I left him then and went to the second floor. I opened up my AOL, found my exchange with Mary, and jotted down her cell phone number. I also sent her a simple email: I lost my phone but I'm going to call you soon.

I didn't know how much she knew or how involved she was, and I was hoping that somehow all of this was Marrow's doing and that she was innocent. She *had* to be innocent.

Then before I could even log off the computer, my email to Mary bounced back and I was informed that this was no longer a valid address, which I didn't like at all.

2.

AT THE HAMPTON INN parking lot, I laid Roscoe across the front seat and covered him with a beach towel I found in the trunk. Then I borrowed his hat to cover my face for the security cameras and crossed the lobby, giving a nod to Halladay's Hampton Inn counterpart, but kept my chin tucked in so he couldn't see my face.

Roscoe's room was on the second floor, and I had the .22 out, leading the way as I opened the door, but the room, with a single queen bed, was empty. I started snooping around and the first drawer I opened had a handful of neatly stacked, crisp, white T-shirts, and seeing his clothing and his fastidiousness upset me. It was too personal. I didn't like learning that Roscoe was neat, that all his neatness had gone to waste, had added up to nothing, and, too, he would never put those T-shirts on again, and feeling like I was about to pitch a faint, I sat on the bed.

I tried to catch my breath, but then I saw him moving around the room, just a few hours before, not knowing he would die soon, and it was like watching a security feed, and I wanted urgently to tell him he needed to be more careful, that he should stop everything he was doing and reverse course before it was too late!

But it *was* too late — I had killed him, unnecessarily; I had lost control during the fight — and panicked with regret, I staggered into the bathroom and drank from the tap, trying to get sane.

Then I picked up Roscoe's toothbrush and felt like Hamlet with a skull.

I almost put the thing in my mouth, as some kind of penance for taking his life, but I knew I needed to get my shit together and so I did a bump of coke.

And a second one for good measure.

That got me back on track, made me numb and single-minded again, and I resumed searching the room. I was going to have to dispose of everything, leave no trace of him, but there might be something here that could help me, and his travel suitcase in the closet intrigued me. It felt a little heavy, and I put it on the bed, but it had a decent lock, and I wasn't sure how to open the thing. Then I remembered *his* switchblade in the pocket of *his* coat, and I cut the bag open and peeled back the canvas flap. Revealed was a tangle of soiled clothing.

He was using the bag for his dirty laundry, which I didn't like touching, it made me squeamish on a number of levels, hygienic and existential, but under his soiled underwear and T-shirts and socks, I found about two thousand dollars cash, a substantial bag of cocaine, a loaded .38, a box of .38s, a box of .22s, and most importantly and most damning, a bag of heroin — I gave it a taste with my finger — along with a baggie that contained a number of clean rigs. All of which confirmed what I already knew: Roscoe had OD'd Ines, given her a hot dose. But it was Marrow who had killed her. Roscoe was just an instrument. And Scruggs was in the clear. His sins were elsewhere, and I'd been a fool.

Then I took out the piece of paper with Mary's number on it. According to the digital clock by the bed, it was 4:43 in the morning. If I tried Mary, I doubted she would answer but maybe she would and if nothing else I could leave a voice mail.

I used the hotel phone to make the long-distance call and it didn't even ring; it went right to a recording that said this number was no longer a working number, just like her email was no longer working. I had no way to reach her now, and either she was involved, or Marrow was keeping her from me, and my growing and frightened sense — or what I wanted to believe — was that she was in danger. The alternative was to think that she was party to having her mother killed. Whatever it was, I needed to get to LA. That's where the answers were.

To speed me along my way, I did two more bumps and called the front desk, pretending to be Roscoe. I told the man who answered that I was checking out, and I got the same question about the card and the bill. "The first card," I said. "The one that made the reservation. Should be my employer's Amex. Langdon. Right?"

"That's the one," said the clerk, and he asked if I wanted to come by for my receipt or have it emailed.

"Email," I said, then added, "but you know, I've been doing so much, I'm all over the place — what day did I check in?"

"Tuesday, sir," said the clerk.

"That's right, Tuesday," I said.

It was now early Sunday morning. I had arrived exactly a week ago, and Roscoe showed up two days later, having driven up from LA with his guns and the drugs, none of which he could have flown with.

"And can I just leave the key in the room?" I asked.

The clerk said that would be fine, and I gathered up the rest of Roscoe's things — from the bureau drawers, the closet, the bathroom — and put everything in his cut-open bag, which I tied off with my belt. Then I left a hundred for the maid, this time out of Roscoe's money, and limped to the Mercedes, wheeling his bag behind me.

3.

I GAVE ROSCOE BACK his hat and drove with him sitting next to me — it had been too risky to move him in either of the hotel parking lots — but I didn't know how much longer my nerves could take it with him riding shotgun. Restrained by the seat belt, he bobbed gently with the movement of the car, which kept making me think he was alive or *coming back* to life, and at every stoplight, I'd feel his pulse, which was nonexistent, and I'd look at the back of his head, which was caved in, and I would reconvince myself that he was still dead.

Finally, after ten gruesome miles like this, I spotted a deserted gas station and pulled behind it. I didn't see any security cameras, moved Roscoe as fast as I could into the trunk, and got back on the road.

I was eager to get out of Washington and forty-five minutes later, I was just a few miles from the Oregon state line. In Oregon, it would be safer to get rid of the body. The farther away from the scene of the crime the better, *should* the body be found.

Then Roscoe's phone rang. I had it waiting on the console in case this happened, and the screen said: *M.* It was nearly 5:30 a.m. The phone had been locked before, but I didn't need a code to answer, just had to swipe, and I put it on speaker and grunted, "Yeah?"

"What's happening? Why haven't I heard from you? Did he show up?"

It was Marrow. I waited a moment, then said, in a hoarse whisper, "You killed Ines."

He was silent, had recognized my voice, and I said, "I'm coming for you."

Then he hung up, and I knew it was a mistake to give him warning — it was a stupid, coked-up macho thing to do — but I figured, too, it wouldn't make much of a difference, unless he left the country, and I hoped to hell he wouldn't do that. But I didn't think he would. He was going to stick around and make sure he got that inheritance money, the twenty-five million. Which I very much wanted to stop from happening, along with wanting to punish Marrow. *Severely.*

I also wanted to get my questions answered, like who was Haze Langdon in all this? Who the fuck was Marrow really? And how much did Mary know and was she in danger?

When I crossed into Oregon, I got muddled looking for the freeway — of course the car didn't have a map and I didn't have access to GPS — and I ended up on the much slower coastal route, the 101, which ran parallel to the ocean. It was still dark out, and there were no stars or moon, and the Pacific was just a great blackness to my right, with a strip of glowing white surf.

I opened the windows — the cold ocean air cleared my head — and as I passed through a town called Cannon Beach, I was able to make out frightening shapes in the water near the edge: gigantic monoliths, the last rocks of the ice age.

Then the road ascended and went above the ocean, along a cliff. Scraggly pines were caught, like ghosts, in my headlights, and to the left of the winding road was the rock face of the mountain, and to the right, far down below, was the sea.

I was the only car on the road at this hour, and then there was a sign, indicating a spot for tourists. It was a little asphalt strip for taking in the ocean view, and I parked the Mercedes in the tiny lot. There was a short wooden fence at the edge, to keep cars from plummeting, and after the fence, there was about six more feet of land before the deadly long drop, at least two hundred feet.

I stepped over the little wooden fence, walked to the edge, and looked down. There was no beach at the bottom, only the white froth of the waves as they hurled themselves against the cliff to no avail, though someday, maybe soon, their hard work will come to fruition.

I went back to the Mercedes and there were still no cars approaching in either direction. There were also no houses on this stretch of scenic road, and so I lugged Roscoe out of the trunk and carried him to the cliff's edge.

I was careful not to slip myself, and then I threw him into the surf with all my strength, and as he sailed through the air, I felt *my* soul go screaming after him, like it was caught on a line attached to his body, and I didn't know this would happen, and I watched him disappear into the sea, swallowed whole, and I teetered there, an inanimate man, a hollow man, unable to move, but then suddenly my soul came rushing back to me, brought in by the wind, with some of the dead man, too, and he had access to my mind and told me that he understood, that he understood everything now.

Reassured and deluded, I got back in the car.

A few miles down the road, I stopped in a town called Tillamook and got my leg fixed at their small hospital. It cost me six hundred dollars cash, and I passed out for a few hours after they stitched me up.

But I was back on the road by noon, with directions to Route 5, which I could take all the way to Los Angeles, all nine hundred miles.

Before I took off, though, I made quick work of it and swapped plates with a car in the hospital lot, using a screwdriver from the trunk. In case Marrow or Haze Langdon had the bright idea to report the car stolen, the Mercedes having Oregon plates would be to my advantage.

4.

I MADE IT as far as Sacramento, pulling into a Motel 6 around midnight.

I had driven nearly five hundred of the nine hundred miles, with just a few rest stops, and was snorting cocaine the whole way.

I had always claimed to hate the drug, but I was justifying and even romanticizing it this time, because as I was doing it, I kept thinking of this scene in that book *Papillon,* where the escaped convict, famously played by Steve McQueen in the movie version, runs through the jungle, chewing on coca leaves for strength. I had read and loved the book when I was in the Navy, and it pleased me in my drug-addled state, as I willed the Mercedes south, to think of myself in the same light as Henri Charrière, aka Papillon, like I was on some kind of heroic mission for which I needed extra-human strength.

But even with all that coke in my system, after ten hours on the road, I began to pass out for terrifying micromoments, waking up with the Mercedes driving itself on the freeway, and so when I saw the Motel 6 sign, sanity intruded, and I got a room.

But once I was in bed, though I was desperate to sleep, I couldn't.

The coke wouldn't let me go under and my jaw was still swiveling like a typewriter.

Then I realized I had a solution and snorted two big lines of Roscoe's heroin off the bedside table. I figured I would need a lot to counteract all the coke, and it hit me hard and sudden, and I fell back onto the bed and saw a gold axe, which cleaved my mind and suffused me with what felt like a solar flare, and then everything went dark, and I fell far inside myself, down a long black tunnel, and I thought, *Oh, I'm dying, I've OD'd, I did too much,* and then I woke up at noon, when the front desk called, asking me if I wanted to check out or pay for another day.

I held the phone to my head and was slow on the uptake. I didn't know where I was and had no memory of the last several days, but then I saw in the sunlight, coming through the curtains, the bag of heroin on the bed-side table and remembered everything like a compressed nightmare, and I told the clerk I wanted to check out but asked if I could have thirty more minutes. He reminded me that checkout was an hour ago but said he wouldn't charge me.

"Very kind of you," I said, and meant it.

I got out of bed, naked, and pissed blood into the toilet. I figured that was my kidney healing from being whacked and stomped and decided to take it as a positive sign.

Then I looked at myself in the large bathroom mirror. My cock I dis-missed as I always did, even though it was dripping blood, and I focused instead on my other injuries:

There were grotesque bruises all over me, a strange mix of colors, red, yellow, green, like rotting flowers under the skin, and my stitched-up leg, wrapped in white gauze, was distended unnaturally, and the long, creased scar where my old kidney used to be looked forlorn, like a barren river, but the scar on my face looked happy. He, poor wormy fellow, felt less lonely for once seeing all this other damage in the mirror, and *my* mood wasn't that bad, either. I realized there was a certain freedom in giving over to my worst impulses. I wasn't trying to hold myself in check anymore with my analysis or my fledgling Buddhism. All that was out the window now. Marrow had taken Ines from me, and I needed to put my hands on him, to balance the scales. He had used me like a pointing dog to kill someone I loved.

5.

By SEVEN P.M., I was crossing the Valley and decided to stop in Tarzana.

I had told Rafi I'd probably be back by the latest Sunday, and it was now Monday night, and I had not been in touch since I lost my phone days before. He had to be wondering what had happened to me *and* how much longer he'd have to look after George, and I was thinking, as I pulled up to his house, that I hoped he wouldn't mind keeping George just a few more days while I attended to some things.

In his driveway, I parked the Mercedes behind Rafi's beautiful old yellow Caddy and limped to the front door. Rafi's house is a single-story, stucco-white box, with white-iron grillwork over the windows. Rafi has lived there a long time with his mother and his companion, Manuel, and he and Manuel have been together at least forty years now, but haven't married because Rafi's mother, who is ninety-nine years old, is a strict Catholic. Regardless, she loves Manuel, thinks of him as a second son and a double blessing, and it was the mother who answered the door standing behind her walker.

She was wearing a faded pink cotton housedress, a white terry-cloth robe, and a pair of gray slippers that looked almost as old as her feet. Her iron-colored hair was in a bun on top of her bowed head and her ancient face was deeply lined but cheery, with large black eyes.

She waved me in. "Entra, entra, los chicos están enfermos."

She speaks English but prefers not to, and my Spanish was good enough to make out something about the boys being sick, and she turned her walker around and led me through the living room, which featured a pink 1950s couch, a glass chandelier that I had to duck, and a small white piano that displayed about a dozen framed photographs of Rafi and Manuel over the decades. Then the mother hung a shuffling left down the carpeted hallway, which was crowded with antique grandfather clocks.

Rafi, probably because he owns a pawnshop, has always liked timepieces of any kind — he trades in Rolexes like they were stocks — and for a while, in the '90s, he had a passion for grandfather clocks, which is why the hallway was lined with them, like coffins with clockfaces.

The mother opened the door to Rafi's bedroom, and Rafi, small, bald, and rotund, wearing shiny blue pajamas, was sitting up in bed, and George was by his side, lying on his belly like a sphinx, like a concubine, and Rafi was stroking him sensuously.

I was wounded by this tableau, and George looked at me in alarm, as if he had been caught with another lover, but then once the shock passed for both of us, George came springing off the bed and leaped all over me like I was a soldier returning home in a Hollywood war picture, and our love was instantly restored.

Then George started racing around the room, dashing about like a madman, not sure what to do with his emotions, and Rafi's mother shuffled back down the hall, and Rafi said, "Thank God, you're here," and I looked around me.

This was clearly a sickroom:

On the big white bureau, which had ornate gold handles, there was an old humidifier shooting steam into the air, giving the room a nice mist, and Manuel, gray-haired and lean, wearing an eye mask, lay in a cot on the right-hand side of the big king bed, and he was dead to the world.

He was curled up fetally, like someone caught napping in Pompeii, and he had orange earplugs stuffed in his ears and was snoring in a congested, sickly manner.

And Rafi, in his enormous bed, with its plush red-velvet backboard, also looked unwell: he was gray and wan, and the rims of his nostrils were an irritated red. By his side was a box of Kleenex, well pawed, and using a remote, he muted the TV. It was an old-fashioned set, resting on a folding bridge table near the foot of the bed, and it was playing a Spanish news channel.

"I've been worried about you," he said. "I've been calling and texting."

"I'm sorry, I lost my phone," I said. "What's going on with you two?" I indicated Manuel.

"We both have this terrible flu. I don't know if it's the one they're talking about on the TV" — he gestured at the set on the bureau — "but we've been in bed for three days and can't walk George. My mother tried — she's the only one not sick, of course — but he pulls too hard, she almost fell, and he won't do his dooties in the backyard, not even number one."

"He's neurotic that way. He must see it as an extension of the house," I said, and George, knowing that we were talking about one of his intimate issues as if he wasn't in the room, stopped racing about and leaped onto the corner of Rafi's bed and sat in front of me, erect and proud in his tan and white suit, like a Little Lord Fauntleroy, and he presented me with one of his toys, a saliva-soaked furry thing meant to have the coloring of a skunk.

"Thank you, George," I said, acknowledging his generous offering, and then I nuzzled his soft white neck with my face and inhaled his odor, which was more beautiful to me than any French perfume, and I thought, *I'm never parting from him again.*

Then I looked up and said to Rafi, "I'm really sorry I haven't been in touch. I couldn't call because I don't have any numbers memorized anymore."

"It's okay. I'm just relieved that you're back." Then Rafi focused his eyes a moment, taking me in, and said, "*You* all right? You look worse than I do. And what are you doing with your mouth? Are you on speed or something?"

"Cocaine. For medicinal reasons."

"Oh, God, what's happening now?"

I told him it was too complicated to go into, and he said, "You haven't killed anybody this time, have you?"

"Of course not," I said, and I thanked him for everything and told him to please feel better. Then I gathered up George and his things and got out of there. I didn't want to burden Rafi with my madness or have him counsel me against further madness.

On the way out of the house, I thanked his mother, and she bent over arthritically and petted George goodbye. Then she looked up at me, smiling. She said, "Un chico hermoso."

"Yes, he's a beautiful boy," I said.

"Ojos hermosos."

"Beautiful eyes?" I asked, and she nodded yes.

6.

GEORGE AND I WENT UP the endless dark stairs to my house and I had the .22 out.

I didn't think Marrow would make a play for me here — he didn't know if I was even back in LA — but I'd had intruders before and was erring on the side of caution.

But nobody was in the yard, and I got my hidden key out from under a planter near the front door. I searched the four small rooms of the house, and it was all clear.

It felt nice to be home, and I went to the bathroom and pissed blood. Then I washed my hands and face in the sink and there were tiny sugar ants scurrying everywhere on the porcelain.

"Hello, ladies," I said, intimately. With all the drought in LA, sugar ants come up the drain of my tub quite frequently in search of water to bring back to their families, and they'll sometimes even spend a few weeks with me and then vanish, and I used to call them "fellas" until I learned that most sugar ants — the workers — are females and that the males don't do much, mostly just lounge about waiting for their wives to come home from work, and they're all ruled — females and males — by a grand matriarch, a queen, who must really be something, seeing how she's in charge of millions of subjects.

It does hit me sometimes that it's not quite normal to live with ants the way

I do, befriending them and all that, but I hate to slaughter the poor things and so I rationalize that it's a rustic kind of lifestyle, and while I was washing my face, trying my best not to drown anyone I knew, I had an idea how to revive myself. So down in the kitchen I filled a mop bucket with ice from the freezer, added some water from the sink, and ducked my head into it. I screamed like I had seen God, but my neighbors down on the street never hear my night screams or my stubbed-toe screams: I'm too far up the hill.

Then I did two more ice baptisms and two bumps of coke, and the combo acted like a defibrillator after having driven four hundred miles that day and five hundred miles the day before *that.* Not to mention the stabbings, the stompings, and the drownings in the days before *that.*

I dried my hair with a towel, changed my shirt, and put on a sweater and my blue-sponge sport coat. Then I tucked the .22 into my waistband, buttoned my jacket over it, and went back down to the Mercedes. I was leaving George home — I gave him a rawhide to suck on to distract him from my abandoning him so soon after our reunion — and I drove the Mercedes over to Skid Row.

I parked on Sixth Street, an old warehouse street, and the sidewalk was lined, from corner to corner and on both sides of the street, with dozens of tents of the homeless, some of whom were walking about, getting ready to bed down for the night, and I flashed to Ines. If I had never found her, she might still be alive.

But I had to fight such thinking and just keep moving forward with malevolent, single-minded purpose, and I removed two remote clickers from the visor over the steering wheel and all the paperwork from the glove compartment.

Then I left the car on Sixth Street with the windows open, the doors unlocked, and the engine running. I threw the papers — insurance and registration — in a garbage can, and I was hoping somebody would take the car for a nice long joyride, maybe even make some money off it, and I limped half a mile to Union Station, where I knew there'd be a taxi queue.

It was close to nine p.m., and I got in the first cab on the line, a green

Prius, and said to the driver, "Take me to the Gelson's on Franklin, over in Beachwood."

Despite the ice dunkings and the coke, I was feeling weak and needed to help my body, which was vibrating with pain all over.

So, with the cabbie running the meter, I went into Gelson's and bought two New York strips, one for me, one for George; a big thing of arugula; a gingerroot; a bottle of Tylenol; and two bottles of grape-flavored Pedialyte. When I was a cop an old juicer and snowbird at the end of his tour — he had managed somehow to put in thirty years on the force — told me that the best thing to take on a bender, whether it was a drug bender or alcohol bender or both, was Pedialyte, which is a dehydration drink for infants with diarrhea that also happens to work restorative miracles on drug addicts and alcoholics.

Back at the house, I gave the driver a nice tip and went up the stairs with the .22 in one hand and my groceries in the other. But only George was there to greet me, and I drank a whole bottle of the Pedialyte, did two lines, and took two Tylenol and an antibiotic from the bottle I had gotten way back in Olympia when I had my leg stitched up the first time. Then I smoked a joint while I cooked the steaks.

Having meat twice in such a short period was extravagant, but these were unusual circumstances, and I thanked the cows — in case it was two different cows — for the gift of their life force in the form of the New York strips, which came out perfect: juicy and fatty.

I put George's steak, which I cut for him, on a plate on the floor next to me so that we could eat together after our long separation, and with my steak, I had a big bowl of arugula with olive oil and salt. I was craving iron, maybe because I was bleeding internally.

George was clearly very happy with his strip — he even seemed to pause a few times to savor the experience — and when we were done, I made a big thing of coffee, which I poured into my thermos.

Then I peeled the gingerroot with a sharp knife, took a little bite, and wrapped the rest in some foil and put it in my pocket. When I'm feeling sickly, I like to chew on ginger, gives me a jolt of energy, like Popeye with his spinach. I also loaded up my jacket pockets with my baton, a small but powerful Maglite, a lockpick, some pre-roll joints, extra ammo, and what was left of the cocaine.

Then I repeated the gag with the ice bucket for a nice send-off, got my spare set of keys to the Chevy, and kissed George goodbye. The .22 was tucked in my pants, and I left the house double-fisted with my two drinks: the second bottle of Pedialyte and my thermos of coffee.

Halfway down the stairs, I paused, and the air was Los Angeles cold, not Olympia cold, and the bougainvillea was a radiant purple in the moonlight.

I said hello to everyone then, the trees, the flowers, the weeds, and I was trying to gather strength from them all, for what I was going to do, and I wasn't consciously looking for a quid pro quo but I did tell them I'd water them tomorrow, which I'm sure they were glad to hear.

In the garage, I put a midsize ladder into the Caprice, angling it from the front seat to the back, and threw an old army blanket in the trunk. I let the engine warm up and sipped some coffee and took a hit of a joint. The Caprice felt so big and earnest after the Mercedes. Then I sipped some Pedialyte and took another hit. I was trying to simultaneously wake myself up and ease my pain, all with the goal of optimizing my functionality.

Then I pulled out of the garage and headed for Haze Langdon's house on MacArthur Drive.

7.

I PARKED UP THE STREET AGAIN and walked back toward the gate. At the top of the long, sloping yard, there was no light over the front door and no cars in the driveway and last time there had been three. The two-door garage, attached to the house on the far left, might have held cars but there was no way to know. I could see little windows in the garage, but they were dark.

Just inside the gate there was an *LA Times,* and I shone the flashlight on it real quick. It was today's paper, Monday, which would have been delivered early that morning, and I looked back up at the house: it had that dead, morose feeling that empty houses get when the humans are gone, like the houses know. Which they probably do.

I went back to the Chevy and got the ladder and the blanket. I limped back to the place under the trees where I had scaled the fence before and just then the rare car went by, but I went flat against the metal fence, in the deep shadow of the trees, and wasn't seen.

There was no way, with my leg all stitched up, I could pull my Tarzan stunt again and so I leaned the ladder against the fence, draped the blanket over the spikes at the top, and was able to lower myself gently to the other side.

Then I yanked down the blanket, rolled it up, and placed it under a tree, camouflaged nicely by the ground ivy. Then I reached through the narrow spacing of the black metal bars of the fence and knocked the ladder over. It was unlikely anyone would make out what it was alongside the dark road, but if they did, they'd just think it was a ladder left behind by some workers.

There were still no signs of life from the darkened house, and I limped up the lawn with the .22 in my hand. Like last time, I assumed that the placard advertising a private security firm wasn't just for show, and I stayed close to the perimeter along the right side, not wanting to trigger any motion detectors.

I went around to the back and there was no theatrical play this night in the glass box. There weren't any lights on, and the pool was also dark, though it glowed in the moonlight, rippling slightly in the cool breeze, and I went over in my mind what I had seen in my previous visit. In that fishbowl living room there had been Hoyt Marrow and Mary and four young men with platinum blonde hair, one of whom was probably Leland Roscoe, and the way the young men had behaved, so at ease in their environment, doing coke, watching sports, it would seem to indicate, on reflection, that some or all of them lived in the house, that maybe it was some kind of compound.

But right now, the house definitely seemed empty. No cars. No lights. And I went back around to the front, then up the left side and hid myself in the shadows between two large trees. It was a little after eleven p.m. now, and I was prepared to wait. From my hidden position, I could quickly walk up to the driver's side of a car, after it was parked, and put the gun on any-one who might come home. And it didn't have to be Marrow. Could be one of the blonde boys or Mary, just someone who could tell me where to find Marrow if I had scared him off with my stupid warning.

And if no one came home that night, I had two other avenues to pursue:

The first was Ines's lawyer. In the morning, I could get a burner phone and call him. I wouldn't go into what would sound like a madman's theory about Ines being murdered, but I could get from the lawyer the address that Mary had given him, the houseboat in Marina del Rey. Maybe that's where they were.

The other way to go, my second option, was to hunt down Haze Langdon. He was a real person in the world with a real name, and he seemed to be funding things. Find him, I find Marrow.

But I didn't like either option — they both would take too much time and I wanted answers now; resolution now; vengeance now — and so I was hoping someone would come home and I could get the jump on them.

My original plan had been to get into the property, force my way into the house, and put Marrow under the gun and make him talk. But that would have been too easy and of course it didn't pan out. And what did I really hope to accomplish? What was my fantasy? It was something like this: Mary was in the dark and by exposing Marrow to her, what he had done to her mother, I could then get at the root of *what* he was and *who* he was; there had to be other things to hang him on, and so I'd put him away, give him to the authorities, with Mary's blessing, and I would destroy him. And if he made things difficult, there was the .22 and the baton and my hands...

Of course, I had fucked up getting him on Ines's murder when I threw away the murder weapon — Roscoe. But I had to just keep blundering forward, that's all I knew.

Then I heard someone cry, "Please help me!"

I didn't believe it, though. Thought it was some trick my mind was playing with the night breeze. But then there it was again. "Please help me!" And it was coming from the garage, muffled, but just loud enough for me to hear.

I ran over to the garage, worried I might set off the security system, but I had no choice, and I peered through one of the darkened windows, which were at eye level, but I couldn't really see anything inside. Then I heard the cry again and held up my small Maglite to the window and in the extra-large, two-car garage there was a workbench area, a car under a canvas top, and then in the other spot, where a car would normally be, there was a very large wooden box, like a storage unit, that went to the ceiling.

I then sidled along the garage windows and shone the light directly onto the box and saw that it had a door in the front, with a metal clasp and a heavy lock, and at the bottom of the door there was a lead panel with a handle.

I stared at the panel uncomprehendingly, not knowing why it was familiar, and then I realized it was the kind of thing you might see in a prison cell, with the panel being able to slide back so you could pass in food on a tray and slide it along the floor. Then I heard the scream again, much weaker this time, followed by silence, and I was certain that it was Mary.

I tried the handle on the garage door, but it was locked.

I then took out the two clickers I had removed from the visor in the Mercedes. One was probably for the gate and one for the garage.

I hadn't dared use whichever clicker was for the gate, not wanting to overtly announce my arrival, but I had thought they might be good to have, and I tried one of them now and made the right choice. The garage door slid up quickly and a light, dangling from the ceiling of the garage, came on at the same time. I felt certain that opening the garage was going to trigger an alarm with the private security firm, but I didn't care. I went to the locked door of the wooden box and screamed, "Mary, are you all right?"

But there was no response, and I squatted down and slid back the panel. I was looking into a dark space, and I shone the Maglite in, and on the floor, caught in the beam of light, I saw a white outflung arm, with the hand at the end limp, the fingers curled and unmoving. Mary's hand! And I screamed out her name again, but she didn't move, and I limped, panicked, to the workbench, grabbed a hammer, and began to bang at the clasp on the door, savagely, until I knocked it off and the lock with it.

Then I swung open the door and was struck by the smell of shit and urine, and in the light that spilled through the door, I saw Mary lying on the ground naked, on her belly, unconscious, but my brain misinterpreted the information from my eyes, because as I turned her over, I realized it wasn't Mary but a small, curled-up old man, with a hairless white body and a shriveled cock with a few gray wisps of hair.

Gently, under the arms, I pulled him farther into the light coming through the door and saw that the man had a tiny face with doll features, which I recalled from the pictures of Haze Langdon at a movie premiere.

He was breathing in a ragged manner, and I figured he must have been crying for help off and on for hours, or days, hoping somebody might hear, and I happened to be there when he tried again. I pulled on a light cord that hung from the ceiling of the box, but the bulb was dead — he had been left in utter darkness; this cell had no windows.

I then knelt down next to him, lifted his head, and said, nonsensically, "Are you all right?"

But he didn't respond, and I lightly slapped his face, but he wouldn't wake, and I wanted to ask him where Marrow was, and I glanced around his little cell, shining my Maglite where the garage light outside didn't reach, looking to see if there was a water bottle or something I could help him with, and in the room there was a cot, a small fridge, a bucket with a toilet seat, and a water cooler with a dog bowl on the floor under the spigot.

It was everything a prisoner might need, but the dog bowl was a sick touch, and then I swept the Maglite up, and on the far wall, there was a locked glass cabinet that seemed to have religious totems, but then as my eyes adjusted, I realized they were dildos and butt plugs, arranged taxonomically by size, and the implements of S&M always strike me, as they did then, as pathetic and banal, and then I heard the front gate opening, and I thought, *Oh, fuck,* and I stepped out of the wooden box into the garage, and a private security vehicle was coming up the long driveway, its headlights filling the front yard with light.

I thought maybe I could get to the perimeter, to the shadows, and I started a limping dash, but the headlights caught me, and the car stopped, and one man came out, slamming his door with urgency. He was thick-bodied, wearing a shiny security jacket, and he read me, naturally, as an intruder, and started reaching for his gun, fumbling with his holster, but I didn't have time to submit and play nice and let him call the cops. I rushed him, screaming, "There's a dying man in the garage!"

He was about twenty feet away and rent-a-cops are almost always alone, it's cheaper, and he said, "STOP!"

But the gun still wasn't out — he had probably never pulled it before — and I screamed, "Don't shoot! Call 911!"

And then his gun was out, but my saying 911 confused him, made him wonder if I was good or bad, and I let him know I was bad, because I threw a running right-handed punch and got him square on the jaw, and he went down to his knees, all messed up, and his gun clattered to the driveway. I quickly picked up the piece, put it in my pocket, and ran down to the gate, which had already closed.

Naturally, I tried the garage clicker to open it, reversing my earlier luck, but then I tried the other clicker, and it worked, and I ran up the street and my bad leg was doing pretty good. I ran all the way to my Chevy and got the hell out of there.

Not a lot had been accomplished, but at least I had met Haze Langdon.

8.

I WANTED TO GET OFF the mountain fast and be lost in the city, and so I took Mulholland to Laurel Canyon Boulevard, which is an easy road to die on if you've been doing coke for forty-eight hours. Or if you're sober. There are no streetlights, it's more of a winding mountain pass than a boulevard, and it cuts down the hill at a fierce angle, replete with hairpin turns and gigantic trees looming on both sides, just begging to be driven into.

Seen from the sky, it would look like a big curvy snake, and to make things really interesting, the oncoming cars blind you, and as I careened my way down the mountain, hoping not to kill anyone, I thought of the night I had followed Marrow and Mary *up* the mountain.

Then I played back, from the beginning, meeting them at the Tower Bar. Like trying to remember where I had misplaced a set of keys, I was hoping to come across some small detail that would lead me to them and while, in the present, I was looking out the windshield at the dark road, I was also seeing myself, ten days before, dropping off the car with the valet and walking up the marble steps of the hotel.

Then I'm talking to the hostess, the one with a gap in her teeth, wearing the gray tunic, and I remembered that she had seemed to know Marrow! She had made an odd face when I told her who my party was and then she wouldn't look at him when she delivered me to their table.

With my coke-addled nerves, I then drove too fast down the hill, headed for the hotel to see if that hostess was there.

And I couldn't shake the feeling that Mary was in danger, serious danger.

It had been a false flag, but what I thought I had seen in that box — Mary on the floor — still felt real to me and was still twanging in my nervous system, like it hadn't been a trick my eyes had played on me. It felt more like a prevision, like how when you see someone on the street and you think, *Oh, there's Bob,* but it's not Bob, but then a block later you *do* see Bob, and that's what it was like, I thought, seeing Langdon on the floor and thinking it was Mary: it was a prevision. A glimpse into the future. Or was I insane? But it didn't matter. *I have to find her,* I thought, desperately.

And I wondered about Langdon. What the hell was he doing in that box? Was he a prisoner? Was it a sex thing gone too far?

I figured that by now an ambulance would be at his house and that the EMTs would probably take him to Cedars-Sinai. Which meant, if I needed to, I could go there in the morning and pay him a visit, and he could point me in the right direction to find Mary. To find Hoyt Marrow. But I didn't want to wait that long for information.

At the bottom of the mountain, I turned right on Sunset, and Chateau Marmont was up on its hill, peering down at the boulevard like an old Hollywood director wearing beautiful clothing from another time, and then a few blocks farther west, in front of the Saddle Ranch Chop House, I found a parking spot on the street, and decided not to bother with the valet stand at the hotel.

When I got out of my Caprice, the Saddle Ranch, built to look like a backlot Western saloon, had ugly music blaring out of its speakers, and the strip was all lit up with its big movie and TV billboards, promoting the latest bodice-rippers and murder-mysteries, and there was a fair amount of traffic for 11:30 on a Monday night, and nearly getting killed, I crossed over to the Tower, an art deco rocket pointed at the moon.

The kid with the forehead pimples who had parked my car last time was hopping into a nice Jag, and I went through the glass doors and up the little marble steps, and the young woman I wanted wasn't behind the lectern. In her place, also wearing a gray tunic and black skirt, was another young woman, this one with red hair pulled tight to her scalp, like a helmet of flame. I went up to her, and she said, "Are you meeting someone, sir?"

"No, not meeting anyone. Just want to sit at the bar," I said.

"We have room," she said. "Follow me."

She led the way into the Tower and the place was quiet, just a few groupings of people in the dim light, and when I looked at the corner where I had met Mary DeAngelo and Hoyt Marrow for drinks, I saw us there, and my back was to me.

Then the hostess delivered me to the long oak bar, and I said, "Wait a moment," and I fished out some of Roscoe's cash and peeled off a twenty, which I passed to her as a tip, and she said, "Oh, thank you, very much," and the bill disappeared into a pocket of her skirt.

"Quiet tonight," I said.

"Yes, it's Monday night," she said, and smiled at me, about to take her leave, but I knew the twenty had bought me some more time, if I wanted it, and I said, "Is your friend working tonight? We met a few nights ago, turns out we both have family in Minnesota."

"My friend?"

"I mean your colleague. She was the host the other night. Very nice gal. I'm blanking on her name, but...uh...she has a gap between her front teeth."

"Oh, Caroline," she said, a little confused.

"Yes, that's right. Caroline Wilson. Very nice person."

"You mean Caroline Zwick?"

"Of course. Caroline Wilson is someone I work with." I smiled at my silly error and said, warmly, "So is Caroline *Zwick* working tonight?"

"No," she said, and I could see I was troubling her. She knew that she had inadvertently given out too much information, so now was the time for me to remove the hook and throw her back. I said, "Well, tell her Paul, with family in Minnesota, says hello. You know there's not too many people you can talk to about Minnesota."

She smiled at me uncomfortably and extracted herself, wondering if Caroline had ever said anything about Minnesota, which of course she hadn't unless I had somehow struck on something true, and I turned to the bar.

There were four people spaced out. Closest to me was a midthirties dyed blonde in a tight blue dress, who might have been a pro, she had that look — her dress was more tight than chic, and she smelled nice but too nice; her perfume cast a wide net. And her posture — shoulders back, breasts out — was proud but inviting; it said: "I'm available but don't be cheap."

Then two bar chairs over from her, there was a New York character actor, a man in his late fifties with sad bug eyes, almost thyroidic. In strange contrast to the eyes, he still had all his lustrous hair, a silver mane, and I had seen him in a lot of Mafia movies, his hair and bug eyes got him the parts, and he was staring straight ahead, looking lonely, a glass of red wine in his hand, and it seemed like he was trying not to notice the pro right next to him. There was a wedding ring on his finger and probably a wife back in New York, but then he angled himself ever so slightly and smiled at the pro; he couldn't help it; he had played too many bad guys who would do just that.

Then at the end of the bar there was a beautiful young Italian couple. The woman was wearing a slinky dress that displayed the appealing braless sides of her breasts, and the man had a five-o'clock shadow and lips like a woman, and I heard him say, "Prego," in a guttural way.

With the Mafia actor next to them it was Little Italy night at the Tower Bar, and the man and woman were probably movie stars back in Rome, though unknown to Americans, but they were certainly beautiful, sleek and elegant, like they had never defecated in their lives and maybe they hadn't. The only things that would come out of them would be cigarette smoke, wine, and olive oil, which was nice for me to think about. Kept them on a pedestal.

Then the bartender, a fish-face in a white jacket, materialized in front of me, but didn't say anything, just put a coaster down and made eye contact, still not talking, but he inhaled, which I think was my cue, and I said, "A Don Julio, ice."

He nodded and went to make my drink, and I thought about things. I had a name now, *Caroline Zwick,* but I needed an address to go with it.

9.

I DIDN'T THINK THE fish-face bartender would sell the address to me, nor did I think the redheaded hostess was susceptible to a bribe.

So I finished my drink and left the bar and went back to my old spot on the sidewalk to the right of the hotel, by the big palm trees. I was just out of the direct line of sight of the valet stand where the captain and his valets hovered, but I was able to keep an eye on them.

My idea was to get information from the pimply kid—maybe he had access to some kind of employee contact sheet or even knew the address himself—but I didn't want to approach him with his captain and the other valets around, and so I was waiting for him to park a car, because I knew how the system worked at the Tower: The valet would jump in the car in front of the hotel, go out the driveway, and make a right onto Sunset. Then they'd drive down a long block, before making a right onto Sweetzer, which goes down the hill, and then they'd make another right, which is De Longpre, and De Longpre runs parallel to Sunset and brings you back around to the rear of the hotel and the entrance to its parking garage, which is beneath the building.

But things were slow right now, and Pimples was just standing there, talking to the other valets, and my body was feeling weird. My bandaged leg was throbbing like a nervy jackhammer, and my head was all big and ponderous, like I was wearing a space helmet. Other than that, I was all right, but to stay on the straight and narrow and keep it together, I chewed some ginger, did a quick bump with my back to the boulevard, and casually smoked half a joint.

Finally, after about thirty minutes, my kid got a car — a black Mercedes SUV. It was almost 12:30 now and soon as he made his right onto the boulevard, I walked about ten feet to a steep, urban staircase that cuts from Sunset down to De Longpre. The stairs are in the shadow of the ten-story hotel, and I limped down the two flights nice and fast.

At the bottom, I was deposited onto De Longpre, which is leafy and residential, and as quiet as Sunset is loud, and I was right by the mouth of the hotel parking garage. It was open and unguarded, and I ducked into it, pretending that I was an employee of the hotel in case anyone should see me. Not that this would work, but I think these sorts of things when I trespass, hoping, almost superstitiously, that my role-playing cloaks me in some manner.

But once I was inside, I dropped the act and climbed the old and narrow garage ramp, which snaked its way up into the building, like a colon, and the lighting was dim, just some fluorescents along the wall. The first level was all full of cars and so I hustled up to the second level where there were a few open spaces, and I thought maybe the kid would park the big Mercedes here. All the cars on this level were vans or SUVs, and I figured this was where they stashed the larger vehicles, and so I stood in the shadows between a bloated BMW and a bloated Lexus.

A minute later, the black Mercedes pulled in next to an Escalade, which was as formidable as a tank, and I made my move. As the kid got out of the Mercedes, I was already standing there in the semidarkness between the two cars, and he did a double take, frightened, and blurted out, "What the fuck?!"

He didn't seem to recognize me, and I said, "I need to talk to you. I'm a cop."

"I didn't do anything," he said. Luckily, he was one of those people whose starting place is guilt and shame, which perhaps explained the forehead acne, and which also made him a good mark, more easily manipulated.

"I know you didn't do anything," I said, warmly, to reassure him. "I need your help with something."

"With what?"

"That's what I want to talk to you about. I —"

"I need to get back to work," he said, cutting me off, his common sense starting to kick in. I was too weird to be a cop and a cop wouldn't be crowding him like this, reeking of weed, but I brought out something that wasn't weird: a wad of cash. A kid who works for tips likes cash. I know I did when I was parking cars.

I said, holding up the money where he could see it, "Here's the deal: I'm a private cop and I need the address of one of your coworkers. She didn't do anything wrong, but she might know where I could find somebody I'm looking for and it's very important." I peeled off five one-hundred-dollar bills from the wad. "I'll give you this if you help me."

He looked over my shoulder, scared somebody might spot us. Then he looked at the cash. This was a once-in-a-lifetime tip — because that's what he thought in terms of, *tips* — and this tip he wouldn't have to share with the other valets. It could be all his. He said, "Whose address?"

"Caroline Zwick's address. The hostess. I'm trying to help a young woman who might be in danger and Caroline could lead me to her."

"Caroline?" The way he said it, I think he knew where she lived.

"Yes."

"You're not a stalker or something?"

"No. I swear. I'm trying to help a young woman who is in trouble and Caroline may be able to help me." I was laying it on thick, but I was sincere. "You know where she lives?"

"But it's late. You can't go there now." His conscience was asserting itself, but there were ways around that. I said:

"I know. I'll talk to her tomorrow. I came here tonight because I thought she was working Monday nights. Listen, you're a nice kid. You parked my car, an old Chevy Caprice, about ten days ago, and I was on the case then."

He remembered me now: the facial scar and the nice tip, the twenty. And I had been somebody who'd gone into the hotel. That validated me somewhat. He looked over my shoulder again. I was lucky it was slow — no cars were being parked — and he said, "You'll really give me five hundred?"

"Yes." I held up the money. "This is yours. And are you working tomorrow night? I'll come back and give you another five hundred. And you can call Caroline in the morning and let her know we talked."

He looked at me: I think my sincerity was coming through, and so I added some vice to help close the deal: "How can you say no to a thousand bucks?"

He looked at me, conflicted. Then he broke, said, "One of the guys used to date her —"

"One of the other valets?"

"Yeah, and I went to a party at her place. I don't remember the number, but it was on Genesee, a block before Melrose. She said James Dean lived there in the fifties."

"North of Melrose or south?"

"Uh…north."

"On the west side of the street or the east side?"

He had to think about it. "West side."

"What kind of place is it?"

"There's a pool in the middle and all the apartments are around the pool, and you can see the pool from the gate. It was the only place like that around there. Old-school."

I handed him the money and he made it vanish, and I said, "I'll see you tomorrow night with the next payment," and of course I would never see him again if I could help it, and I started walking away then and just kept going, all the way to my car and all the way to Genesee.

I parked the Caprice and walked up the street and two blocks north of Melrose — not one block, but the kid's memory had been pretty good — I found the apartment building where you could see the pool from the gate.

And the gate, which kept one from entering the complex, was a series of ten-foot-high metal bars, like prison bars but painted white, and built into the middle of the bars was an iron-mesh door, also painted white, and it was locked.

I looked through the bars and the amoeba-shaped pool was beautiful and iridescent. It glowed blue with underwater lights and lapped in the wind and threw undulating light beams onto the walls. It was like peering into an aquarium, but this wasn't a school trip. Caroline Zwick was listed as 2C in the directory, and I took out my lockpick.

10.

IT WAS A TWO-STORY BUILDING, with both stories wrapping around the pool in the middle, and up close it was evident that the place had seen better days: the dusty potted plants were in a state of despair; the pool bottom was chipped and flaking like an asbestos ceiling; and the concrete around the pool from years of earthquakes and baking in the sun was buckling and cracking.

But, still, it was a charming little kiss of old Hollywood. Maybe James Dean *did* stay here a moment.

Poolside, there were some metal circular tables and chairs, all painted white and chipping, and the second-floor apartments were reached by an outdoor staircase, painted blue. The staircase led to an exposed walkway and a balcony that wrapped itself all the way around the building. And all the apartments, on the ground floor and the second floor, looked onto the pool, like a motel.

There were twenty-four units in all, and each one had a large outer-facing window, and the windows were covered with a variety of curtains and blinds. About three-quarters of them showed no light. It was a little after one a.m. and most everybody was asleep or not home.

But Caroline Zwick was home.

Or I hoped she was.

From the ground floor, I could see a light in the window of 2C.

I padded up the outdoor staircase and crossed in front of her large window.

The thick white curtain made it impossible to look in, but at the edge of the window, near the front door, the curtain hadn't been pulled entirely flush and there was a sliver of an opening that I could peer into.

I looked around — the place was dead — and then I put my eye against the window like a real Peeping Tom, and in that sliver, I could see that she was on a couch across from the window, wearing pajama pants and a T-shirt. She was sitting with her legs folded under her, and she was staring down at her phone, that universal posture, which was convenient since she was oblivious to me, engrossed as she was by the glowing rectangle. She was also smoking a joint. A girl after my own heart.

Then I straightened up and knocked at her door. I heard her say, startled, frightened, "Who's there?"

I said, "I'm with a private security firm. Your boss at the Sunset Tower Hotel is in trouble and we need to speak."

"What?"

Her voice was closer now, she was on the other side of the door, and the peep-eye darkened, and I angled myself so she couldn't see my scar.

"I'm with a private security firm and your boss at the hotel is in trouble. You've done nothing wrong, don't worry, we just need to talk. Let's talk down by the pool, at one of the tables."

Then she opened the door a crack with the chain in place and she had a bottle of Mace pointed at me. She said, "Who the fuck are you? I'm going to call the fucking cops!"

The sensible thing for her would have been not to open the door, but I had intrigued her talking about her boss and her place of employment — how did I know where she worked? — and I quickly took out two one-hundred-dollar bills and held the cash near the chain. I said, "This has to do with a situation at the hotel. Come down and talk to me by the pool and I'll give you three hundred more. Bring your Mace, your phone, whatever makes you feel comfortable."

Then I quickly folded the two bills over the chain before she could say anything and walked down to the pool. I sat at one of the metal tables where she could see me from her window, and I hoped to hell she wasn't calling the cops.

So I sat there waiting, wondering if my gambit would work and what I might say to the police if they did suddenly show up, and I knew I didn't have a good story, in fact, I didn't have any story at all, and I was about to bolt, but then I saw Caroline's door open, and I watched her make her way down to me. She had a winter coat on and a knit hat, and in her hands were her phone and the Mace.

She stopped about six feet from the table and stood in front of me. She was tall and beautiful and young, twenty-four or twenty-five, and her face was in shadows, but I saw the fetching gap in her front teeth, and she said, accusatorily, in a low voice, "How did you get in here?"

"The door in the gate was propped open. Probably for a take-out delivery or something."

She looked over at the gate; what I had said was probably often the case. Then she whispered, angrily, "Tell me what's going on."

I put three hundred dollars on the table and said, "I'm a private cop. You and I met ten days ago. I was a customer at the bar, and you took me to a couple in the far-right corner and you seemed to know the man. A big guy, very tan, early fifties, named Hoyt Marrow, and he was with a young woman, early twenties, green eyes, skinny."

Her eyes widened in fear, something I said had rattled her, but she still wasn't calling the cops and she still wasn't spraying me with the Mace. She regained some of her composure and said, "What's this have to do with my boss?"

"Nothing. I'm sorry. But I need to find this man."

"You bullshitted me?"

"Yes, because the young woman, who was with that man, is missing and I think she's in danger and I want to help her. I'm working for her mother. So do you know Hoyt Marrow?"

She took an angry step, like she was going to leave, then turned back. "I can't believe this. I remember you. How did you find me?"

"The internet."

It was a lie of course, but a believable lie, and she shook her head, sick with the world, sick with how we've all lost our privacy, but she still wasn't leaving and she still wasn't calling the cops. Something was keeping her around. She knew something.

I said, "I'm sorry to barge in on you like this, I really am. I just need to find this man, and anything could be of help."

She stared at me wondering what to do and started pacing in a jittery way, probably a little stoned from the joint she had been smoking. Then she stopped and said in a whisper, "I don't know him. I know *her*." Then she sat down at the table, grabbed the three hundred dollars, and slid her chair back to keep me at a safe distance.

My heart pounding, I said, "You know Mary?"

"She had a different name. But we all did. Nobody used their real name. I knew her as Alicia."

"Where was this?"

"Is she really in danger?"

"Yes," I said, urgently. "How do you know her?"

She lowered her head and wouldn't look at me and she was very beautiful in that moment of her life: skin glowing with health, lustrous hair spilling out from her winter hat, high cheekbones. All that and the gap between her teeth, which somehow amplified her loveliness, but around her mouth lines had begun to form, lines of fear and worry. I said to her bowed head, "I'm sorry if this is painful, but anything you tell me might help me find her. *Please.*"

Then she looked up, ready to confess something. "I was with this modeling agency for a little while, except it wasn't. That's just the way they got you in. It was an escort service and the bastard that ran it owned a boat and sometimes he would take clients out with a few girls." Then she looked down, ashamed. "That's where I met her. Just once. On the boat. But I liked her."

"Who's the man that owns the boat? Not the man at the bar? Not Hoyt Marrow?"

She looked up at me. "No. His name's Jack Kunian."

I was pretty sure I knew the answer, but then I asked, "Where does he keep his boat?"

"Marina del Rey."

I was getting close now, real close. "When did you meet her? When were you on the boat together?"

"Last April." It was around then that Ines had reached out to Mary, and Mary had given a boat slip as her address to the lawyer writing up the will.

I said, "Does Kunian live on his boat?"

"Yes."

"Does Mary live on the boat?"

"I don't know. Maybe. I was only part of the whole thing for two months — it was like I got hypnotized — but she said she'd been working for him for a long time, since she was a teenager." Then she put her face in her hands and started crying. "I never told anybody this, and now I told you, a stranger."

"What you told me is going to help me find Mary."

She nodded and kept crying into her hands. I let her go on like that for a little while and then I asked her if she knew the anchorage for the boat in Marina del Rey and sure enough, she still had it in her phone.

11.

AT THAT TIME OF NIGHT, it took me only twenty minutes to get to the ocean.

From Washington Avenue, I made a right onto Admiralty Way, which loops around the enormous marina, one of the largest in the world.

Kunian had his boat anchored at the Esprit slip and in front of the slip there was a parking lot, about half full. I parked the Chevy and separating the lot from the docks was a large gated fence, with plenty of cameras and a nice little topping of razor wire.

I wasn't hoping for much, but I got out of the car—it was cold by the ocean—and I checked out the lock on the gate. As expected, it was too formidable for my little doohickey—there was too much money on the other side of that fence—and so I went back to the car and waited. The parking lot was well illuminated, and on the dock, on the other side of the razor wire, there were light poles every thirty feet or so.

I was there just a few minutes when a private security vehicle did a loop in the parking lot and I ducked down, unseen. Then it exited the lot and made a left back onto Admiralty Way, heading for the next slip, and I checked the time. It was nearly two a.m., and I figured they would probably hit this lot every twenty minutes or so, which was something to keep in mind.

To stay sharp, I lowered my driver's-side window, which let in a rush of frigid air. It was probably in the thirties this close to the water, and there were all sorts of little chiming sounds and metal clicking sounds coming from the rocking boats, and the cold air felt good and smelled good, with just the slightest bit of kelp to it, and on the other side of the fence, amid the many motorized yachts, there was a large grouping of sailboats, and they looked like a cluster of knights waiting for their orders, their white lances pointing expectantly at the black sky.

The minutes ticked by and to help pass the time, I smoked weed, sipped coffee and Pedialyte, chewed ginger, took two Tylenol, and snorted a little cocaine. Then sure enough around 2:20 the security vehicle made its next pass, and I was starting to feel that I might have to call it a night, that there was a good chance that nobody who lived on their boat would be coming home late. It was LA and people went to bed early. If they were night owls, they tended to do their heavy drinking at their house. Or on their boat. Not out at the bars.

But then I told myself that the gods had been good to me that night. They gave me Pimples who gave me Caroline who gave me Kunian. Now I just needed the gods to give me somebody to get me through that gate, because I really needed to find Mary, and so I waited and prayed for a night owl who owned a boat on the Esprit slip and who had been doing their drinking elsewhere. Or if it wasn't a night owl, it could be someone coming in on a late flight from an exotic locale, because if you lived on a boat that's the kind of thing you specialized in: late flights and exotic locales.

And that's who showed up.

Sort of.

Around 2:30, a silver two-seater Porsche Carrera zipped into the lot, and it looked like there was only one person in the car, the driver, which was good. A couple might have been too difficult, too many potentialities for resistance, and I looked over at Admiralty, there were no cars passing and the security vehicle was roughly ten minutes away. I hoped.

Then the driver of the Porsche, a tall man in a gray overcoat and a pilot's uniform, got out of his car and retrieved a rolling bag from his trunk, as well as his pilot's cap, which he put on because of the cold wind. He started walking toward the gate and I got out of the Chevy and limped over to him quickly.

"Excuse me," I shouted, friendly, and he waited for me. He was a man in his late fifties with a skeptical look on his face, and I came right up to him. We were about fifteen yards from the entrance to the dock and I turned my back to the gate and the cameras and showed him the .22 with its long, dark barrel, like a finger of death. I said, "I need you to take me onto the dock."

This specimen of American male in front of me had made a little fairy-tale life for himself — jet planes, Porsches, boats — to match his looks: he had 44 regular shoulders, gray sideburns, a chin that was used to getting what it wanted, flinty blue eyes, and breath that smelled of whisky. Uncon-sciously, perhaps, he had modeled himself after *Playboy* magazine's idea of the perfect man, circa 1978, which would have been his formative years, and to complete the package, he had a nice big Rolex on his wrist. He was probably ex–Air Force, most airline pilots are, and he had a notion of him-self that didn't like having a gun pointed at his belly. He said, maybe a little whisky-brave, "This isn't happening, asshole. Fuck off."

Then he looked like he wanted to try something, maybe swing his bag at me, and I said, hoping to impede that impulse, "You fuck around, I'll shoot you, get in my car, drive off, and you're dead. Or very badly injured."

At the end there, I let a little bit of the nice guy slip out *and* the truth, which was a mistake, made him not take me seriously. But the most recent bump of coke had hit me funny, had loosened me up a little and messed with my filter, and I had genuinely thought that if he gave me too much trouble, I could just shoot him in the leg, and he said, "Get the fuck out of my way."

Then he pushed me with his free hand to get past me — he was an arro-gant son of a bitch to put his hands on a man with a gun — and I hated to do it, but I had to appeal to his intelligence, and so I raked him across the face with the barrel of the .22, catching his cheekbone good and carving a groove in his nose, and instead of anger there was a look of humiliation and shock in his eyes: it had been years since he had been hit and he had forgotten how much it hurt, and then I slapped him across the face with my left hand, to complete his submission, and I shoved the gun hard in his stomach and said, not fucking around anymore, "I'm a sick person, you dumb fuck, but take me to your boat and you'll come out of this alive. Play the big picture and you win. You're too smart to die in a parking lot. Now, fucking move."

He grabbed his nose, looked at the blood in his hand, then started walking to the gate with a hitch in his step. I followed close behind him, the gun in my pocket, and I was pleased: he had broken pretty easily. He fumbled with his keys at the gate, his hands were trembling, and I put the barrel of the gun into his kidney. I said, "You can land a jet plane, you can open a gate," and he got it together and we were onto the dock.

I glanced back then at Admiralty Way and the security vehicle was just approaching. The timing had been perfect, and the pilot led me along the concrete dock, past all the monstrously expensive sailboats and yachts, and the people who owned these things were the people who had too much.

The pilot's boat was a little smaller than most, it had just one level, with a partially exposed cockpit on the roof of the front cabin, but it was still quite impressive and was called *The Great Escape,* which made me think of Steve McQueen again.

I said, stepping onto the boat, "You live here alone? No wife or girlfriend?"

"Nobody," he said, barely audible, and he kept holding his nose, and we went into the cabin. There was a nice lounge and galley, and on the port side, there was a set of wooden steps down into the belly of the ship, which led, I figured, to the sleeping berths. He faced me in the lounge, his rolling bag by his side, and said, disgusted with himself, "Now what?"

Gun pointed at his belly, I said, "Believe it or not this isn't a stickup. I'm not going to take anything from you, not even that nice Rolex," which I did somewhat covet, "but I do need something from you. Something to tie you up with."

He lowered his head, none of this made sense, but because he was good around the boat and handy, he had a big roll of gray electrical tape and a carpenter's razor in his large chest of tools, and I had him take me to the toilet, which on a boat, of course, is the head. I thought that would be a good place to stash him — it was belowdecks, next to the master bedroom — and I wrapped him up pretty good. I taped his ankles together, taped his mouth, and secured his wrists to the pipe under the sink. The carpenter's razor made my work easy, and when I was done, he was pretty well immobilized and wouldn't be able to free himself.

I didn't want to humiliate him further, but having drunk coffee and Pedialyte, I desperately needed to urinate, and so I relieved myself into the metal toilet, angling my back to him so he wouldn't have to see my dispirited cock.

"I'm so sorry about this," I said to him, and I meant it, and there seemed to be less blood in my flow, though I may have been lying to myself, and when I finished and was all zipped up, I looked at the pilot and he was utterly morose.

I said, "In a little while, I'll call marina security and let them know you're in here. Shouldn't be too long." He looked at me, then looked away, more a wounded child than a wounded man, and I *did* intend to let someone know he was in there. Strange things happen to people when they are left tied up: they often don't make it.

I closed the door to the head and listened outside a moment to see if he was going to thrash about. But I didn't hear any noise, and I pitied the man and thought to do tonglen for him but then didn't feel worthy of anything Buddhist, of anything decent. *What's happening to me?* I wondered, finally pausing for a moment. *I just kidnapped and beat an innocent man.*

Dr. Lavich, I figured, would say I was in a state of regression, and that was probably right. The dual training wheels of my analysis and my nascent Buddhism had gone flying off back in Olympia, and I was on my own now: violent, regressed, brokenhearted.

I went up the stairs to the lounge. Whatever was going on with me, I told myself, was irrelevant. There was no stopping now, and I got off the boat and the sharp, cold wind felt good. Anything numbing was good. In my pockets were the electrical tape and the carpenter's razor in case I needed them.

It took me a little while to find Kunian's slip, but then I did, and Kunian's boat was quite a lot bigger than the pilot's. It was a triple-decker yacht, with the bridge on the third level, and was called, fittingly, for a floating brothel: *The Pleasure Seeker.*

It was about seventy-five feet long and there were lights visible in the windows of the middle-deck cabin, though I couldn't see what was behind the windows at that angle, and I kept walking, like I was headed to my own yacht.

I walked for a few boats, passing in and out of the shadows between the light poles, and at the end of the dock was a clear view of the channel and beyond that the Pacific, a monstrous void. I had yet to see another person since I had first gained entry with the pilot, and most of the boats, I presumed, were empty, and the people who did live on a few of the crafts were most likely asleep.

I stared out at the water — some distant tankers with their lights on were at the edge of the black horizon like fallen stars — and I went to do a bump of cocaine to give me energy for whatever was to come next, but even getting a small bit of blow up your nose in a strong wind is impossible, though that didn't stop me from trying three times.

So after that bit of private, humiliating slapstick, I managed to rub a bunch of it into my gums, which was better than nothing, and then I doubled back to Kunian's boat. Some light spilled onto *The Pleasure Seeker* from the closest light pole, but the yacht was mostly in shadow.

I stepped onto the large craft and immediately squatted down by the back railing, wanting to go small. It hurt the stitches in my right leg to squat like that, but I counted to thirty, waiting to see if I had triggered anything, and nothing happened. In front of me was a dark, glass-enclosed cabin and to the right of the cabin was a white fiberglass staircase to the middle deck.

I stood quickly and went up the stairs, the .22 down by my side.

At the top there were sunbathing lounges and then another large glass-enclosed cabin, which was all lit up from within, and I was looking into a spacious lounge and galley, where three men were sitting around a built-in table, playing cards and drinking.

The table had banquette seating and there was one man at each end of the table and a man in the middle, who was boxed in and dealing the cards. They were all very large men, and I opened the glass door to the cabin, waved the .22 at all three of them, and said, "I need to speak to Jack Kunian."

12.

WHEN I SAID "KUNIAN," the two flanking men — dark-haired, swarthy bruisers, wearing tight-fitting blazers — looked at the guy in the middle. *Kunian.*

This was my meat, and he wasn't pretty. He had a big bald dome, a fringe of dyed-black hair, a lower lip like a slice of cow liver, and to top it all off, his bloodshot brown eyes were even more thyroidic and protuberant than the actor's back at the bar.

I pegged him at around sixty years old, and he was squat and obese, at least 300 pounds, and his big belly was up against the table. He was an anti-Buddha, and he wore a white shirt and a blue blazer made from enough cloth to be a bedspread, and in the front pocket of the blazer was a pack of cigarettes. A big tabby cat, also obese, walked along the back of the banquette behind Kunian, then stopped behind its master and licked a paw.

Kunian looked at me with disgust and said, "What the fuck are you?"

His voice was a smoker's rasp and then the bruiser on the right was suddenly reaching under his jacket and drawing a gun across his body, and I got lucky and shot him where I was aiming, which was the back of his hand, and the cat shrieked and leaped off the banquette, and the bruiser dropped his gun, a snub-nosed .32, and pitched forward onto the floor.

The bullet had gone through the hand and into the banquette, and there was a bullet-hole stigmata in his palm, dripping a lot of blood, and he was saying, "Fuck, fuck, fuck," and then the other bruiser charged me — he wasn't carrying—and I was so screwed up on coke and everything else that my aim was good that night, perfect even, and I stepped back and shot the second bruiser right where I wanted, which was in the knee, and he came up short, fell to the ground, and I went over and smacked him on the back of the head with the butt of the .22, putting him down for a little nap. Then I looked up and the fat man, Kunian, was trying to get out of the banquette, but not moving too fast because of his girth, and I gave the other bruiser, who was in a state of shock, his own nap-tap, and Kunian still hadn't squeezed himself out, so I picked up the .32, shoved it in my pocket, then sat at the table across from Kunian, and he stopped moving. The .22 in my hand was pointed in his general direction, and everything was nice and quiet now, like a hush after a storm.

On the table were the playing cards, a crumpled pile of bills, a large, heavy bottle of whisky, three tumblers, and an ashtray with a lot of crushed cigarettes, lumped together like maggots. Then the cat, blasé, like nothing had happened, leaped back onto the shelf of the banquette and brushed itself against the back of Kunian's head and his fringe of poorly dyed hair, which was more eggplant-purple than black.

"You're lucky you didn't shoot my cat, you son of a bitch."

"I'm a dog person, but I wouldn't shoot a cat," I said.

His bloodshot bug eyes stared at me like I was crazy, then he said, "I don't know why Benny sent you. All I have on hand is thirty thousand cash. That's it. You can have that, but the rest can wait till Friday, like I already told him." He looked at his men on the floor—they must have been his security detail—then he looked back at me, mystified. "I don't understand this violence. Makes no sense."

I didn't know who Benny was, of course, but I said, "Thirty thousand sounds good. But I have some questions for you first. Is Mary DeAngelo on this boat?"

His big head sucked backward into his fat neck, then jutted back out. "Mary DeAngelo? What the fuck are you talking about?"

"I'm talking about Mary DeAngelo. Is she on this boat? If not, where can I find her? And do you know who Hoyt Marrow is?"

"You're not with Benny?"

I didn't say anything to that, but he figured it out for himself, and he said, "Then I'm not talking to you, you fucking bastard," and he suddenly reached behind his head real fast, grabbed the cat, and threw it at me, an orange hissing bomb, with paws flailing and fangs bared. It was mesmerizing, like waiting for a fiery comet to land on your head, and then all at once it was on me, its claws slicing open my left cheek and my scar, and somehow it leeched onto my face, tearing at me with its claws and spitting on me, and I felt like the fucking cat was going to kill me, and I grabbed it by its neck and threw it to the ground.

Then Kunian was above me, swinging the big whisky bottle, which I blocked with my left arm and the heavy bottle didn't shatter, but the force of the blow sent me back into the banquette onto my right elbow. I thought he was going to swing the bottle again and brain me with it, but he was going for my gun, which I had dropped to the table fighting off the cat, and I lunged out of the banquette and tackled him, and we tripped over the first bruiser I had shot and we fell to the floor, rolled once, with Kunian ending up on top of me, all 300 pounds, and he had the gun in his hand.

So I squeezed him around the neck — keeping him tight to me like a lover — which kept him from rising up and shooting me, and I could smell cigarette breath and baby powder and something intimate and disgusting that smelled like hummus.

But then he broke my hold and lifted his enormous torso and swung the gun around, and I gouged one of his bulging eyes and he screamed, and I wrenched the gun from his hand and smacked him with it across his face, and he rolled off me, howling.

I staggered then to my feet and kicked him hard in the gut, which stopped his crying as he sucked for air, his chest heaving like a bellows.

I stumbled over to the table, unstoppered the whisky bottle, and with shaking hands poured myself a slug. Kunian was still hyperventilating on the floor, and the tabby, no worse for wear, shot down an inner staircase to the next level on the boat, while blood dripped off my cat-ripped face.

A little shook-up, I grabbed a twenty from the table and tried to stop the bleeding with it like the twenty was a tissue or something, but then my head cleared, and I realized that was disgusting—money is dirty—and I went into the galley, walking kind of dizzy. I soaked a paper towel with some water and dishwashing soap and held it to my face like a compress.

I checked on Kunian and he had rolled onto his back and was staring at the ceiling, his chest still going up and down pretty fast, but he was kind of serene now, like an animal that's gone off to die and is hiding somewhere, just waiting for it. The eye I had gouged was already closed and swelling and his nose was dripping blood from when I had smacked him with the gun.

The two men on the floor with him were starting to rouse, and so I trussed them up with the tape that I had taken from the pilot's boat, and with the butt of the .22 I hit them on their occipital bones to put them back to sleep.

Then I stood over Kunian and pointed the .22 at him. I had thrown the compress to the floor and blood dripped from my face onto his white shirt. His one eye looked at me with hate.

"Where's Mary DeAngelo?"

"Where she is, you can't find her, you sick fuck." He was a tough, sneering bug at my feet, a fat Napoleon type used to being in charge, and his ugliness was part of his power, made him want to bring everyone down to his level.

"What's that supposed to mean? Why can't I find her?"

"She's dead, asshole."

I kicked him hard in the side where he'd feel it in his lung, and I screamed, "Don't fucking lie to me!"

He was gasping again bad, his heart ready to blow, and I bent over and put the .22 against his forehead. His hateful eye was scared now. He didn't want to die and he didn't want me to hurt him anymore, and he mumbled, in pain, barely a whisper, "I'm not lying. I swear. She's dead."

I looked at him. He *wasn't* lying and I felt a weakness come over me, like a diabetes thing, and the room started to tilt and act funny. My prevision had been true, and I went over to the table and sat down, thinking I might faint. Then I poured myself another slug and that steadied me. After a minute, I got up and nudged Kunian hard with my foot. "Sit up."

He didn't move. "Sit up!"

He rolled to his side, he was too fat to get up any other way, and then, keeping the .22 on him, I helped him stand. But I didn't need the gun. He was no threat now. He was weak and didn't have any more cats to throw at me.

I shoved him into the banquette and poured him a big tumbler of whisky. He lifted it to his mouth with two trembling hands and drank from it like a beggar with a bowl of soup. I got a fresh paper towel to hold to my face and gave him one for his nose. I sat down and pointed the .22 at him.

The whisky seemed to fortify him a little and he lowered the glass to the table and said, "I don't understand what this is all about. I don't understand what you're doing here." He licked some blood off his meaty lower lip and put the paper towel against his nostril and held it there, and we made quite the pair, holding paper towels to our faces.

"You don't have to understand," I said.

"Then what do you want from me? What's it going to cost me?"

"Just answers."

He crumpled up the paper and let his nose drip blood. He said, still used to being top dog, "Okay, answers I can afford."

I let him think this was a negotiation and said, "How do you know Mary's dead?"

"Her friend called me. Her best friend."

"Who's that?"

"Katarina."

That name meant nothing to me. I said, "How do you know this friend's telling the truth? What did she say happened?"

"She said Mary OD'd —"

"Can you trust her? You sure she isn't lying?"

"She wouldn't lie about something like that. She and Mary were like sisters, and I was close to both those girls. *I raised them.*" He said that with feeling, maybe what he thought was a paternal feeling, but this man was a pimp and a sociopath. One of those monsters that walk among us, filled with self-hate, consuming everything in their wake to numb their pain. Then he lifted the whisky back to his mouth, his hands still trembling, and looking at him was like looking in a fun-house mirror. The image was distorted but it was me just the same. The difference was I didn't want to be a monster. I had awareness. Which made things worse. All the bad karma and none of the fun.

"You sure she said it was an OD?"

"Yes, I'm sure. Why do you care? What's she to you?"

I didn't answer that. I took the paper towel away from my face — the bleeding had stopped — and I sipped some whisky, trying to think. Could Mary really be dead? Had Marrow used the same method on mother and daughter? Had he taken Mary out with an OD and made it look like an accident so that he could inherit the money from a dead wife?

I said to Kunian, "When did this Katarina call you? When did this supposedly happen? Saturday? Sunday?" Ines had been killed on Friday.

"No. She called me like two weeks ago, told me that Mary took a hot shot on New Year's and never woke up." Then Kunian lit a cigarette, his hands were still shaky, but his strength along with his confidence was starting to come back.

"This friend called two weeks ago? Said Mary died on New Year's?"

"Yeah, New Year's. If she hadn't stopped working for me that never would have happened. I don't let them get too wild."

I almost shot him right then, but instead I stood up, feeling icy and sick. Something bad was coming into focus. Something even worse than what I thought had been going on. I said, "Do you have a picture of Mary on your phone?"

"Yeah."

"Show me."

He took his phone out of his inside jacket pocket and started going through his pictures. Then he turned the thing toward me, and I kept the gun on him, but got close enough to look. It was a stylized photo, like a bathing-suit pinup for a 1950s calendar, and the beautiful young woman in the phone was not the person I knew as Mary DeAngelo, but she did look just like Ines.

13.

"Now show me Katarina."

He played with the phone and turned it around.

I took it out of his hand and was looking at the girl I had met in my office and had drinks with at the Tower bar: the beautiful flapper with the off-kilter eye. I expanded the photo — which was the same kind, a retro fifties pinup look — and sure enough her eyes were blue. She must have been wearing green contact lenses when I met her.

I put the phone down on the table and started pacing, all agitated and fucked up. I had been played real good, and Kunian watched me, looking for an angle in my weakness. The cigarette was giving him new life, and even with all that extra weight, he was a street-rugged old boy and hadn't gotten to his place on the criminal side of the food chain — sitting in his yacht — without mettle, without brains.

I stopped pacing and said to him, "Why did you have those kind of pictures of the girls?"

"What's the difference?"

"Just tell me, asshole."

"They were for the website."

"Your escort site?"

"Yeah. I showed you the tame ones. I didn't want to get you excited. You seem jumpy, coked-up."

He was trying to needle me. "I am coked-up. So don't fuck with me."

"Okay, I won't fuck with you, but my men need medical attention. They're going to bleed out."

"No, they won't. This is a .22. Really only fatal if I shoot you in the head or the heart," and I aimed the gun at both places on his body and he didn't like that, and I saw the fear in his working eye again. He couldn't figure me, and I said, "Are you going to keep answering my questions or do I put a bullet in your brain?" I placed the barrel of the .22 on his forehead.

"Okay, okay," he said, compliant, and I pulled the gun away.

"How long did Mary and Katarina work for you?"

"Six years."

"How old were they when they started?"

"I don't know. Seventeen, eighteen. They were homeless junkies, living right over there in Venice, and I cleaned them up, let them live with me here on the boat, and turned them into real ladies. Gave them books to read. Took them to museums. Gynecologists. Everything. I treated them beautifully."

This guy was nuts and he was proud of himself, his own sick version of *My Fair Lady* playing in his head. He probably even thought the girls loved him, which explained the dyed fringe of hair; the absurd, deluded vanity.

I said, "When did they stop working for you? You said they left you."

"You asked about Hoyt Marrow. He stole them from me."

"Tell me what you know about Marrow."

"You know what," he said, like he was giving me a gift, "you're better than these two schmucks. Supposed to keep me safe, but they're useless." He gestured toward his men with his cigarette, then crushed it in the ashtray. "I could use you. Pay you nicely. Look at you. You're in rags."

"I don't work for pimps."

"Bullshit. Everybody's half pimp, half whore. We all answer to somebody. Even me." He said "whore" like "hoor," and I put the barrel of the .22 against his forehead again. "I'm not looking for a job. Tell me about Marrow."

"Okay! Okay! You could kill somebody doing that."

"Tell me about Marrow."

"That's not his real name."

I pulled the gun away, said, "Keep going."

"His real name is Dave Exel."

"Tell me everything about him."

But then Kunian clammed up again. His ego was just too big for this, he'd been on top for too long, didn't know when to cut his losses anymore, and he said, snarling and threatening, "You know what, sicko, get off my fucking boat, you have a face I won't forget," and I felt a siren go off in my head, and since he wasn't scared of my gun, I took my baton out and smashed him in the ear. He screamed and started rocking in the banquette, holding his ear, moaning, and then the two schmucks on the floor were starting to wake up and moan, and the place was like an ICU of my own making.

I taped shut the mouths of Kunian's men — so I wouldn't have to hear them — and my nerves were twanging like crazy. I was cat-scratched, sleep-deprived, coked-up, bleeding internally, and I had been set up by two con artists to put the finger on Ines and have her killed.

So I threatened to hit Kunian again, swinging the baton at his head and coming up just short, like I was some kind of torture freak, and I said, "Tell me about Exel."

Kunian, who had raised his arms to ward off the blow, wouldn't look at me. He put his hand back over his bloody ear, like that would keep it safe, and said in a monotone, "Exel was my old partner. Fifteen years ago. Then we split."

"What happened?"

I saw him glance at his empty whisky tumbler. Playing both good cop and bad cop, I filled his glass and pushed it toward him. "Go ahead."

He kept one hand on his ear and with the other hand, trembling, he lifted the whisky to his lips and drained the whole thing. Then he stared at the table, in shock.

I said, "Why did you and Exel split?"

"He killed his boyfriend."

"Boyfriend?"

"He swings both ways. Always rough. Men or women. This one he killed."

"Why did he kill him?"

"He was high and screwing the kid and strangling him at the same time. Then he passed out." He looked up at me. "That's what fucked him."

"What do you mean?"

"Didn't have time to get rid of the body. Cleaning lady called the cops."

I fed him another half tumbler of whisky and he put it down like water. I said, "Then what?"

"He made bail and disappeared. For fourteen years. Showed up a year ago, the bastard, with a new face and a new name and plenty of money. Can I smoke?" He was all submissive now, asking permission to smoke.

"Sure."

He lit a fresh cigarette, and he closed his good eye in relief as he inhaled. He took his hand away from his ear and let it drip blood, but at least his nose had stopped bleeding.

"How did he come back with money?"

"Got his hands on an old queer movie producer down in Mexico. Became his master."

"Master?"

"You know, S&M. Findom or whatever the fuck they call it. Guys like that turns them on to have their money stolen."

I'd heard of findom, and it explained Haze Langdon's part in all this. He was the piggy bank, literally. I said, "So Exel came back to LA, with his new face, new name, and was living off the old man?"

"Yeah," he said, holding the glass like it was his best friend and I poured him two more inches. The bottle was almost empty. He threw his medicine down and said, getting more voluble with each drink, "Yeah, he was living off the old queer, then started running a stable of pretty boys."

"If he was running boys, how did he steal the girls from you?"

"His Scientology bullshit. He gets people to do things. Everyone becomes his slave, but they think it's a family. He's always been like that. Half Jim Jones, half pimp." He was suddenly very drunk now and he smiled at me. The booze and the pain had taken another turn: he was almost in a good mood, and I was his buddy.

"Marrow's a Scientologist?"

"Not really. He learned stuff from it."

"How?"

"He came here to be a movie star and joined Scientology, like every other jerk. This was back in the eighties and even the Scientologists kicked him out, but at least he made it in acting. Except it was porn, the dumb fuck. Then he started *hooring* himself to the rich men around town. He was lucky he didn't get AIDS."

"How did you meet him?"

"He smartened up and got on the right side of the bed business, which is when I met him. Mid-'90s. And we teamed up. He was a good recruiter. He had the looks. I had the brains."

I poured him another two inches, which killed the bottle. He put that down, then swayed a little, closed his good eye.

I said, "Why did he steal the girls from you?"

He kept his eye closed, exhaled a cloud of smoke, and said, "Out of spite because I wouldn't team up with him again. I knew he'd self-destruct."

"I went by the old man's house, the movie producer," I said. "Exel isn't there. Where would he go if he's not there?"

Kunian opened his drunk eye, said, "I have no idea."

Even though we were all friendly now, I put the barrel of the .22 against his forehead again. He said, urgently, but slurring more, "I don't know. Take your finger off the trigger. Jesussh."

I pulled the gun back. "Are you sure?"

"I'm sure. I don't know where that bashtard goes, what he does. He took the girls from me, got 'em in his little cult, and that was the lasht I saw of that piece of shit."

I believed him. Then I said, "Call Katarina."

He looked at his watch. It was a little after five a.m. "She won't answer."

"Doesn't matter. Call her."

He found the number.

"Put it on speakerphone."

He did and the call went straight to that familiar recording, the one that lets you know that this number is no longer in service. I had him try the number he had for Exel/Marrow and we got the same thing. They had gone to ground. Kunian wasn't of much more use to me now, but I asked him again, "You sure you don't know where he and the girl would be?"

"I'm sure."

I hit him in his good ear not that hard but hard enough to scare him into telling the truth, and he said, desperate, "I don't know where they are. I told you!"

He was holding both ears now and I looked down at him and he was a mess. I was in the man-breaking business that night. Then I asked him, "Who's Benny?"

That really made him clam up and I had to hit him again, much harder this time, and I found out that Benny was a lieutenant in the Jalisco Cartel, based in LA, and Kunian worked for them. He had his name on the yacht's paperwork but in truth he leased the boat from the cartel and did runs for them on occasion, and Benny was his handler, which explained Kunian's half whore, half pimp philosophy. And the way I figured it, Kunian had a three-pronged business plan: drugs, sex trafficking, and blackmail, since that went hand in hand with high-end prostitution: wealthy johns are frequent extortion targets.

At this point, Kunian, who was on the verge of passing out, had told me all he could, and so I had him take me to his safe in the master bedroom.

The thirty thousand he had mentioned earlier was more like sixty thousand — of course he had lied — and feeling like I had earned it, I put the cash in a black garbage bag to take home with me. Also in the safe were two foil-wrapped bricks. I did a small taste test: one was cocaine and one was meth. I put the bricks on his bed and left them there.

Then I taped Kunian up on the floor, and by 5:20, I was back in my car in the parking lot. I did a large bump to clear my head from the whisky and got onto the freeway. At that hour, there was no traffic, and I made one stop.

In Crenshaw there was a 7-Eleven with a pay phone outside. I parked the car a block away — so no cameras would connect me to the call — and when I picked up the phone it had a dial tone. Keeping my back to the camera over the front door, I called 911 and told them there were several dead bodies, cartel-related, on two yachts at the marina. I gave them the boat names and slip numbers and hung up.

Of course, there weren't any dead bodies, but I wanted to make sure they took the call seriously. The pilot would tell them a story, but I was hoping the coke and the meth on Kunian's bed would tell a bigger story, because I wanted Kunian out of commission. I didn't want him looking for me and his sixty thousand. At least not right away.

I got back on the freeway and by six, I was home. George jumped all over me, and I told him I had met a very mean cat, which I knew he would be sympathetic to. Then I went into the bathroom, said hello to the ants, and put a big square bandage on my face. I was going to have a scar over my scar.

Then I went into the bedroom, hid the money in my closet, and emptied my bulging jacket pockets of the baton, the tape and the razor, and all the guns I had collected — the .32 from the boat and the .38 from the rent-a-cop at Langdon's house. The .22 I kept in the waistband of my pants, and I took George for a walk. He had been cooped up since we came back from Rafi's.

14.

WE HEADED UP BEACHWOOD in the direction of the Hollywood sign.

It was predawn, but still very dark: the sun wouldn't be out for another hour.

My immediate plan was to walk George, sleep a few hours, then get a phone. I'd call Ines's lawyer and tell him what was safe to tell him, without incriminating myself, if that was possible, and after that I'd go to Cedars-Sinai and talk to Haze Langdon, see if he could put me onto Marrow and Katarina's trail.

Hoping to get the coke out of my system so that I could sleep without having to snort heroin, I took George on the big Belden Drive loop, which eventually comes back around to Beachwood, and my mind wouldn't stop racing and I thought about everything, the whole strange case, telling it to myself, like a story:

Ines, on Facebook, reaches out to Mary in April of 2019.

Mary still has a Facebook account and is living on the boat with Kunian.

Ines tells her about the possibility of inheritance someday, and Mary gives the address of the boat to Ines and the lawyer.

Then sometime after that, Marrow poaches Mary and Katarina from Kunian, and they leave the boat and move in with him, probably at Haze Langdon's house on MacArthur Drive.

Meanwhile, Mary stays in sporadic touch with Ines, but doesn't tell Ines much or anything about her life. Then Ines goes off the radar in early November when she gets gangrene in both legs and has to be double-amputated.

So they don't speak for almost two months and then Ines's mother, Mary's grandmother, dies on Christmas Day, and Mary is informed, probably by the lawyer. The lawyer then tells Mary he can't locate Ines and asks her to try.

But she can't get ahold of her, either. Ines doesn't have a phone.

But Mary needs to let her mother know what's going on.

Needs to let her know that she's going to inherit a lot of money.

And maybe Mary thinks her mother will help her out and if that happens maybe she can get out of the lifestyle and get away from the Marrows and the Kunians... her mother owes her...

But she's not sure how she can find Ines. She doesn't even have a picture. But then she sees my name in the newspaper, because of Bill Lusk jumping off the bridge. And she remembers my ludicrous name: *Happy Doll*. Her mother had told her to find me if she ever needed help. *Happy Doll, a sad doll, who calls himself Hank*. And so she thinks that maybe this guy could find her mother. *He knew her*.

Then she tells her best friend, Katarina, all this, because she tells Katarina everything. Katarina is her sister. They have been together since they were homeless.

And so Mary is planning to reach out to me, but then she dies on New Year's and never writes me, and she's gone. Dead. And she didn't inherit her mother's money, but she got all her afflictions: homelessness, prostitution, drugs, and it ends with an OD. Probably at Haze Langdon's house. But Marrow doesn't call 911. He doesn't want anyone coming around: he can't be looked at too closely.

So Mary's death isn't reported and he gets rid of the body. He's not going to make the same mistake he made fifteen years ago. Then Katarina tells Marrow about Ines and the dead grandmother and the inheritance, and one of them gets the bright idea that Katarina can become Mary. They have her social security number and Katarina knows her life story backward and forward and who's going to question it? The only family Mary has is Ines and they have plans for Ines. From the start she's to be killed.

But first she has to be found.

And so they use Mary's plan to hire me, and Katarina gives a great performance, screwy enough to seem real, and I take the bait. Then Marrow gives me the once-over at the Tower Bar, figures he can dupe me, if he needs to, and so they send me, the fool, the clown, up to Olympia to find Ines.

Which I do.

But then I gum things up, make them rush. I tell Marrow that Ines has been double-amputated, and that I won't leave Olympia until Mary shows up to help her.

But Mary can't show up. She's dead and if Katarina comes as Mary, Ines will know it's not her daughter. Even if she hasn't seen her for years, she'll know. And their plan had probably been to wait for me to leave town before they killed Ines, because I would have no reason to question it if I got the news that she had OD'd. It was the fate of nearly every junkie.

But I tell Marrow I won't leave town until they show up, that Ines can't be left alone, and I also rattle Marrow, pester him about his phony name, and he starts thinking that maybe the whole thing is going to fall apart. So he gets impatient and makes a mistake: he has Roscoe kill Ines while I'm still in Olympia, while I'm at the hospital getting stitched up.

Then they don't hear from me.

I disappear because I'm busy getting stomped and drowned and half killed.

But Marrow doesn't know this, and he gets paranoid. Thinks I'm onto him more than I am, and he sends in Roscoe again. But Roscoe is no assassin. He has the toys, the silenced .22, the .38, but he's too pretty, just a kid, and he's probably not just Marrow's "assistant" but one of his boys, one of his prostitutes, one of his little cult members.

And Roscoe, following Marrow's orders, had probably, in the past, gotten rough with some of his johns — the closeted married men Marrow would deem vulnerable to extortion — but killing me in my hotel room is on another level of criminality, and the kid fails.

Then I foolishly tell Marrow I'm coming for him, which spooks him into hiding, and when I get back to LA, I blow up his nest at Langdon's, which leaves him even more exposed and vulnerable. But he still thinks if he takes me out of the picture that he and Katarina can make the inheritance scam work and that the twenty-five million will set him up better than Langdon ever could.

But I was definitely in the way of all that happening, which is why when George and I had finished our walk and were heading up the stairs to my front gate, two men, platinum blondes, came flying out of a parked BMW with guns in their hands.

Marrow's other boys had found me.

15.

I DIDN'T WAIT TO SEE what they were going to do with those guns, and I swung the gate open, dragging George with me, and two shots slammed into the fence — they were muffled, silenced .22s, like the gun I was carrying — and I limp-raced up the darkened stairs and George was fighting me. He wanted to go *at* the attackers, and I pulled out my .22, while turning partway, and they were ten steps below us in the shadows under the trees and I fired at the blonde in the lead. But the gun jammed, I must have fucked it up hitting Kunian's men, and then I got shot in the neck, and George cried out, either shot or I stepped on him, and I let the leash go and leaped down the stairs at the men, like going off a high dive, and beneath me they were stacked up like bowling pins, and then I landed, violently on the first one, driving him into the second one, and that blonde fell backward and broke his skull on the hard steps, the thud was grotesque and definitive, and we were all tumbling together. Then I was lying across the first attacker — I had ridden him like a sled — and the three of us were in a heap at the bottom of the stairs.

I passed out for a minute, then rolled off the two men. I got out my Maglite and checked for pulses. The one in the back was dead and the one I had landed on was unconscious. It was around 6:20 and still very dark out, and the street was quiet. No one had heard anything. The confrontation had lasted twenty seconds.

I felt my neck. It was bleeding nicely but it was a superficial wound and I felt dreamy and silly. I was stunned, in shock, but then George came racing down the stairs to me and that got me straightened out. Using the Maglite, I inspected him: he was uninjured.

I put him in the house and got the .32 I had taken off Kunian's man. I also grabbed the electrical tape and razor: there was just enough tape for one more trussing. I went down to the guy who wasn't dead and put the flashlight on him. His right shoulder was jutting out funny: it was probably broken. I slapped him to consciousness and said, "Where's Hoyt Marrow?"

16.

MARROW AND KATARINA WERE out in the desert, in Joshua Tree.

I had to show the blonde the .32 to get this information, but he came out with it quick enough, and then I had work to do. I patted him down for other weapons, but he was clean, and I pocketed the two guns on the ground, which my assailants had dropped when I landed on them like a 190-pound grenade.

I had the living blonde stand up, and he realized then that his friend was dead, and he looked away. As a defense, he lapsed into confused self-absorption. He said, "I think my shoulder is broken."

"Good," I said. He was another pretty boy, like Roscoe, another male prostitute playing with guns and out of his league. Except he was younger than Roscoe, probably all of twenty-two, a real baby. I had him hand over his phone and the keys to the BMW and we went down to the street. The BMW was a black four-door and I hit the key fob and made him lie on his left side across the back seat. He was tall and had to bend his legs to fit, and he said, "What are you going to do with me?"

I said, "Don't worry about that right now," and I put the gun under his chin to keep him behaving, and then I trussed up his hands and feet. He was grunting with pain because of his shoulder, and so I taped his mouth shut. Then I taped his head to the seat, facing the windshield, and got out of the car and looked around. Luckily, I'm on a dead end, a cul-de-sac, and the street was still sleeping.

I popped the trunk in preparation and went up the stairs and through the gate. I did two bumps of coke, told myself I was a superman, and lifted the dead man onto my shoulder for a fireman's carry.

Then I scrambled through the gate, nearly fell down the steps, and tossed the dead blonde into the trunk. I had never thrown dead men in trunks before and now I had done it twice in the last forty-eight hours.

I slammed the trunk closed and looked around again. There were two dwellings on the cul-de-sac that could have seen me dealing with the blonde men. One was an apartment over a garage and the other was an old brick four-story apartment building, with a unit on each level. That morning all the apartment windows were dark and the window in the garage apartment was also dark.

I started to head for my stairs and just then a young woman, a brunette in her late twenties, came out the wooden front door of the brick building. She was wearing black jogging leotards and a purple hoodie and had earbuds in for music. I had seen her around for a few months and she stared at me with surprise. I had never been on the street at 6:30 in the morning before and she had the look of a daily early-morning jogger. But I gave her a friendly little wave and she gave me a small nod in return, then set off on her run, and I was pretty sure she hadn't seen anything. But I had gotten lucky.

Then I went up the stairs and into the house. I taped up my neck with another white pad to match the one on my face, and then I pissed some more blood.

I washed my hands and when I looked in the mirror, I didn't recognize the ugly man who was playing me. I shrugged that off and went back downstairs. For weaponry, I repocketed my baton, figuring it was always good to have, and decided to go with Roscoe's .38, which was plenty of gun, but then, on a whim, I took out my old ankle holster. The .32 fit in it perfectly, and I strapped it on, and the whole thing — gun and holster — hid nicely under my pant leg.

It wouldn't hurt to have two guns, one in my pocket and one on my ankle, and I was about to leave, and George knew it and looked at me anxiously. To reassure him, I knelt down and kissed him goodbye, but I felt bad doing it, like I would taint him, and I withdrew from him and locked the front door. *How can he still love me?* I thought. *I keep killing people.*

But as I walked down the stairs, I still believed on some level, as a way to rationalize my actions, that I was doing all this for Ines, out of some twisted notion of justice, but the real reason, the unconscious reason, was much more selfish:

I simply had to burn this whole thing down so that someday I could start again.

17.

I PARKED THE BMW behind the 76 gas station at the corner of Franklin and Beachwood. The sun was starting to come out, and I turned to the back seat and removed the tape from the blonde's mouth. I pointed the .38 at him and said, "What's your name?"

He hesitated then said, "Alex. Is my friend dead?" His eyes were scared and with his head taped to the seat he was forced to look at me.

"You know he's dead."

"What are you going to do with me?"

"I'm not going to do anything with you. How did Marrow know I was back in LA?"

"Something went wrong at the house, and he figured it was you."

"The old man's house?"

"Yeah."

"Is that where you live? Where you all live?"

"Lately."

"You're like a family?"

He didn't know how to answer that and didn't say anything. I dropped it and said, "So what's the protocol now, Alex?"

"What do you mean?"

"After you killed me are you supposed to call Marrow or text Marrow or what?"

"Call."

"And who makes the call? You or your friend?" I nodded in the direction of the trunk.

He hesitated to answer. I said, "Which one of you is the leader?"

He still didn't say anything, which was some kind of misplaced pride, and I leaned over the seat and put the barrel of the gun against his forehead.

"Eric would make the call. He was in charge."

I withdrew the gun as a reward. "And if you made the call what would happen? Would that tip Marrow off?"

"It might. He'd ask for Eric."

"Okay. We won't call, then. What kind of place is it in Joshua Tree?"

"Tell me what you're going to do with me."

"I told you. I'm not going to do anything with you. I'm going to bring you back to your boss. We're going to drive to Joshua Tree. So what kind of place are they staying at?"

"You're not going to kill me?"

"No, why should I? What kind of place is it?"

"A ranch house."

"Where's it located? Near the town?" I'd been to Joshua Tree a few times. It was all desert, with one quarter-mile strip of stores.

"It's not near the town. It's in the middle of nowhere."

"Neighbors?"

"Why?"

"Because I like to know things. Just answer the questions." I put the .38 against his forehead again. He exhaled nervously and I could smell his breath: it was sour with fear. I repeated myself: "How close are the neighbors?"

"Not close. Like half a mile away. But you can't see them."

That made sense: when you had a house out there the whole point was isolation. I said, withdrawing the gun, trying to picture things, "Why can't you see the neighbors?"

"The house is set way back from the road and it has a big metal fence.

And it's right next to the park. So all you see is empty land." In Joshua Tree there's an enormous national park full of the endangered Joshua tree, which explains the name of the town, and the trees gather there, each one lifting its bristly arms to the sky.

"Who's with Marrow? Katarina?"

"Yeah."

"Anyone else?"

"Ray."

"Who's Ray? Another blonde rent boy?"

He closed his eyes with shame. He was a prostitute and a wannabe killer, but he was kind of an innocent, a dumb, pretty innocent. He said, embarrassed, "Yeah. A rent boy."

"He and Marrow have guns?"

"Yes."

I asked him for the address, and he said it was in his Waze.

"What's your code?" I held out his phone.

He told me the code and I put the tape back over his mouth.

18.

Waze said it was a 140-mile trip that would take roughly three hours and ten minutes.

I hadn't slept for twenty-four hours, but resolute, I went into the 76, got a large coffee, two hard-boiled eggs wrapped in cellophane, which I was surprised they carried, and a Gatorade, since they didn't have Pedialyte. The cashier looked at the bandages on my face and neck but didn't say anything.

Back in the car, I did a big bump of coke, lit a joint, and started driving east to the desert, directly into the sun. I thought of putting on the radio, but it didn't seem like the time for music: there was a dead man in the trunk.

As I drove on the 10, a brutal, ugly freeway, I was holding out a sort of sexist hope that Marrow had forced Katarina to do all this, that she was so under his sway, so Stockholmed, that she really had no choice. Which wasn't implausible. Marrow was her pimp. His psychological hold on her would be practically lobotomizing.

And I guess I wanted to think of her in this light — as a victim — so that I could add another layer of rationalization for what I was going to have to do.

Which was to kill Marrow.

And the new layer of rationalization was that killing him would free Katarina.

All of which meant that I was now *intending* to commit homicide.

Everything before had been self-defense. Could almost be explained away. But not this.

This would be execution. And my fall would be complete.

I knew, *distantly,* that the way out of all this was probably the Buddha's teachings on emptiness and the turning of the dharma wheel, in which he explains how our suffering can be transformed, how hate can become love and how violence can become peace, but I hadn't gotten that far yet in my studies.

19.

ABOUT A HUNDRED MILES east of Los Angeles, the ugliness of man — the destruction of the natural world that radiates out from the center of LA — finally began to wane. The endless industrial complexes that feed the monster city had petered out and the thick blanket of inland smog had cleared.

And the old vast sea bottom, the Mojave Desert, took over.

I exited the freeway and headed north on Route 62, and the last gasp of industry — what heralded our entry into nature — were the far-reaching windmill fields, which go on for miles. The windmills — and there are thousands of them — are painted white and are several stories high. They stretch across the flat desert land and look like pinwheel crosses marking the graves of giants.

After the windmills, the road ascended for a few miles, up and over a stretch of the red San Jacinto Mountains. Then the Mojave flattened again, and the GPS said we were twenty-five miles from our destination.

We had been on the road for about two and a half hours — it was close to 9:30 — and the morning light, without the filter of smog, was crystalline and there was a whole other dimension of color to the world, a vibrancy and radiance that I wasn't often exposed to. The rust-red boulders out in the desert seemed to hum in their place on the spectrum and the blue of the sky was so pure and unsullied that I felt a kind of primitive awe.

It was almost like I had forgotten why I was out there and then Alex's phone, which was resting in the center console and open to Waze, started ringing.

It said, *No Caller ID,* and I didn't pick up.

I was certain it was Marrow.

He must have tried the boy in the trunk first and gotten no answer.

Then the phone stopped ringing, and I hoped this meant that Marrow was still in Joshua Tree. He'd only now be certain that his little team had failed, since they weren't answering their phones, and if I was lucky, he wouldn't be on the move just yet. But he might be very soon, and that had always been a possibility — that I'd get out there and he'd have slipped away again.

I picked up the phone to get a better look and the GPS said I'd be there in thirty minutes.

Any element of surprise I might have had was definitely lost, and I was very concerned that they were going to flee. But the speed limit was fifty-five and I couldn't risk going any faster: I had Alex taped to the back seat and there was a corpse in the trunk.

Finally, we passed through the main drag of Joshua Tree — two stoplights, a liquor store, a bar, a health food store, a gas station — and five miles after that little burst of civilization, we turned onto the first of a series of dirt roads that took us farther and farther out into the wilderness.

The last dirt road was more or less a long private driveway — there were no other houses off it and no visible neighbors — and after a bend in the road, about fifty yards away, there was a high four-sided wall of rusted corrugated metal, with an opening in the middle, large enough for a car to pass through. Beyond the opening, I could see part of the ranch house, a fragment of its orange adobe skin.

We rolled slowly forward, and it was a very isolated spot, desert and Joshua trees all around, and I wondered if the real Mary was buried somewhere out here.

Then I stopped the car about twenty yards from the entrance and got out, staying low behind my open door. I pulled Alex out of the back and cut the tape around his ankles so that he could walk. His hands were still secured in front of him, and I also kept the tape on his mouth. He was a little wobbly and I was a little wobbly, and I got behind him, with the .38 in his back.

"Let's go to the house," I said, and I put my left hand on his neck, and he tried to say something. I told him to shut up and gave him a little push with the .38, and he started walking up the dirt road and I stayed right behind him, using him as a shield. The sun was still low in the sky, but bright, and everything was very still and quiet. Then an enormous hare, like a mini kangaroo, took flight as we approached.

I stopped five yards from the gap in the metal wall and could see that inside there was a large sandy courtyard with planted cacti and a fire pit, and on the right side of the courtyard, parked under a canopy, was a black BMW SUV, which was good: they were still home. And straight ahead, about thirty yards away, was the house itself, a simple adobe rectangle with a shaded front porch and rocking chairs. By the front door was an enormous picture window, but the sun glinted off it, and I had no idea if we were being watched or not, but I assumed we were.

I called out, "MARROW, LET'S TALK!"

But I got no response. The house was still.

I squeezed Alex's neck again, stayed small behind him, and said, "Keep moving, but slow."

In all fights the key is distance.

Control the distance — set the terms — and you win the fight.

And you either want to get in close where you can do the most damage or you play it defensive and keep your counterpart far away — you use the jab, the claymore mine, the drone, and you take them apart slowly, while staying safe.

In this situation, though, defense wasn't an option, but I could still control the distance, which was my goal: get close to Marrow and be the better man.

And I figured it was to my benefit that he had surrounded himself with amateurs. I had already bested three of them, and so he didn't have an advantage in numbers with the other rent boy who was in there somewhere. Also, Kunian had said that Marrow was rough in bed, which usually meant cowardice *outside* the bedroom.

So I was cocky approaching the house, never a good thing, and just as we passed through the opening in the metal wall, Marrow and Katarina, unarmed, stepped out onto the porch, and there they were.

I squeezed Alex's neck and we stopped moving, and it felt like a victory just to see them. That I had caught my prey. Marrow was in jeans and work boots and a leather jacket, and Katarina was in a long flowing dress, over which she was wearing the same cardigan sweater she'd had on the day I met her.

I almost wanted to call out to her, *I'm here to free you,* but then something glinted on the roof, and I realized I had made a terrible miscalculation: I thought that Alex might be of some value to Marrow, which was fatally naive, because the thing that glinted on the roof was a man with a rifle, and he had very good aim because he shot Alex in the head and my poor shield fell to the ground, and I lifted up the .38 toward the roof, but much too late, and a bullet punched into my left shoulder, and I dropped my gun and went straight to the dirt, and then there was another shot, but it missed, and I rolled to my left, behind the metal wall, gunshots blasting into it.

I stood up and ran, but not for the car — that would give the shooter a sight line down the road — and so I ran along the corrugated wall. I had to find cover, but I couldn't swing my left arm and that slowed me down.

When I got to the corner of the wall, to the right, about fifty yards away, was a large outcropping of rocks and to the left, about a quarter mile away, was a house, but I'd never make it there. So I had to get to the rocks. If they got close to me, I might be able to get them with the .32, but only at close range, the gun had no other use.

I ran for the rocks and then I heard them behind me, Marrow and the man from the roof, another one of Marrow's platinum blondes, and they had handguns by their sides and were trotting after me, calm but lethal. The neighbor's house in the distance — the off chance of someone seeing something — was keeping me alive, otherwise the blonde would have brought his rifle.

I ran as hard as I could, going past Joshua trees, impassive and unconcerned, and Marrow called out, "Doll, stop!"

Then I was at the rocks, great big tan boulders, with a crevice in the middle. But there was nothing immediately that I could hide behind, and so I had to get to the other side, find something there, and I scrambled up the crevice, and a shot blasted right next to me.

Marrow and the blonde were almost at the base of the outcropping and the rocks at this angle weren't visible to that house, so they felt free to fire, but then I was over the edge, and scrambling down the other side.

There was a boulder about twenty yards from the bottom that I could get behind, make my stand there, but then as I hit the flat ground, suddenly everything gave out — my dead arm, my stitched-up leg, my utterly depleted body — and I fell to the sand.

I tried to get up, but couldn't, and then Marrow and the blonde were coming down the rocks. The sun was behind them, and I saw Marrow smile. I wanted to reach for the .32 but I had no strength; I was paralyzed. I didn't know why but I had fallen short right at the end — Ines would not have her justice, after all — and then Marrow was above me eclipsing the sun, and he kicked me in the head twice. The first kick I saw a sheet of blood and had the thought that it was a terrible shame I had so rarely felt happy in life and the second kick brought on a sudden blackness.

20.

I CAME TO AS I was being dragged, under the arms, to the back of the house.

Ray, the last of the platinum blondes, was the one who had me, and we were being followed across the dirt yard by Marrow, who was dragging Alex, and then there was Katarina, bringing up the rear, and by her side, in her listless hand, was the .38 I had dropped.

My heels were kicking up dust, and I could feel the weight of the .32 in my ankle holster, still hidden under my pant leg. They hadn't checked me for other weapons because they were amateurs. Deadly amateurs.

But this was not the time to reach for the .32: the blonde had me under the arms — there was no way to break from him — and there was also searing pain coming from the area of my left shoulder, where I had been shot, and I looked down and I hadn't noticed it before but there was a scorched hole in my jacket and a widening stain of blood.

We came around the back of the house, which was more private than the front, and the blonde propped me, in a sitting position, against the high metal wall, which circled the whole property. My legs were stretched out in front of me, and my ankle holster looked to be a million miles away. When I made my move, it was going to have to be perfect: I'd only have one chance. Katarina saw that my eyes were open and said, "He's conscious."

Marrow dropped Alex to the dirt, stood in front of me, and took a .45 out of his pocket. He said, "You've done so much damage to me, Mr. Doll," and then he raked me across the face and the bridge of my nose with the barrel of the gun, just like I had done to the pilot. *Karma.* In Buddhism they say that whatever you make someone else feel, *you* will feel someday. Well, that someday had come around fast, and I grabbed hold of my nose, got blood all over my fingers, and said to Marrow, "Nice to see you again."

Then I turned to Katarina, who was to my left, but she wouldn't look at me, and I said, "You, too, *Mary.*"

That got her to look and her strange eye focused on me, and Marrow bent over a little, put the barrel of his gun under my chin, and lifted my head up. His leather jacket was tight with all his bulked-up muscles, and I thought if I reached for the .32 now, he'd blow my head off.

"What happened to your face?"

"You just hit me with your gun."

"No, this." He ground the barrel of his .45 into the dirty, loosened bandage on my cheek.

I flinched with pain and said, "I tried to get friendly with a cat."

He decided to ignore that and said, "Where's Eric?"

"The one you sent with Alex? He's in the trunk of the car."

"Dead?"

I didn't answer.

Marrow commanded the blonde, "Go look," and this one, Ray, was just like the others: about six feet, surfer-handsome, midtwenties. They could have all been brothers. So far three out of the four were dead.

The boy left, and Marrow straightened up and pointed the gun at my head, which made me think of Kunian, *more karma,* and I stared into the black eye of the barrel.

Still no chance at the .32.

Marrow said, "Who have you talked to? The cops? What do they know? Are they on their way?"

I could see that he was very frightened. His eyes were yellow, and under his tan, his reconstructed face was gray with fear. He had been running from himself for a very long time, hoping not to be punished, and he knew, devious creature that he was, that his string was running out and looking at him, I realized, was like peering into another fun-house mirror. The image was distorted but there I was again. I had also been running for a long time. I said, "What are you so scared about, Exel?"

He looked at me shocked. Couldn't understand how I would know his real name. "I know everything about you," I said. "I know everything you've both done." Then I looked at Katarina. "How could you do that to your friend, *Katarina*? Kill Mary's mother?"

"I didn't think it would happen like this," she said, barely a whisper, then looked at Alex dead on the ground.

"What was *supposed* to happen? Only Ines would die?" But there was no point shaming her, really. She was still just a child. She'd never had a chance.

She said, waving the .38 in her hand, mindlessly, "I didn't understand. I didn't!"

Marrow said to her, "Shut up," then pointed his gun at my head again. "How do you know that name Exel? Who have you been talking to?"

"I know you killed your boyfriend years ago, *Dave,* and ran away, wanted for murder." I turned to Katarina. "Did you know that? That he killed one of his boys?"

Then I had a flash of insight, along the lines again of how we're all doomed to repeat the past — Marrow, me, everyone, and call it what you will, samsara, repetition compulsion, insanity — and I said to Katarina, in a rush, hoping to rattle Marrow and give me a chance at the .32, "And he killed Mary, too. Was having sex with her but got too rough because he always gets too rough, because he's weak and has to prove he's a man. He told you, though, it was an OD, didn't he? Then he told you, you could get her money. But he killed your friend, Katarina, just like he killed before."

A look shot between them — I had hit on it. Marrow's face gave it away and Katarina knew it was true!

But just then the blonde came back and said, "Eric is dead in the trunk."

Marrow said, pointing at me, "Shoot him."

The blonde, obedient, took out his gun. "Are you sure?"

"Yes, kill him and then we're out of here."

Marrow, the coward, couldn't do it himself, and the blonde, Stock-holmed like the rest of them, lifted his gun, and I closed my eyes, girding for the impact, and I could hear my heart pounding in my ears like the giant's footsteps from my childhood nightmare — he was still looking for me and had been all my life — and then there was a deafening shot, but not into me, and I looked up and the blonde was falling and Katarina was holding the .38 out, having just fired, and Marrow, enraged and without thinking, shot her in the chest, and she went down, and he stared at what he had done, incredulous, and I dove then for my ankle holster and Marrow turned to kill me, he realized now he could do it himself, but I had the .32 in hand and I fired, and a black hole appeared in his right cheek and for a moment there seemed to be a stunned and terrified recognition in his eyes.

Then he crumpled to the ground, dead, and the blonde was dead, and I went over to Katarina and her eyes were open, blinking, and her hands were folded calmly, like in prayer, over the large hole in the middle of her chest, and we were surrounded by all the dead bodies, our tragic little battlefield, and blood was seeping through her fingers, but she didn't seem to notice, and her strange eyes were very blue, the bluest they would ever be.

I sat down next to her in the dirt and cradled her head, and she said, "It's not bad, right?"

"Not bad at all," I lied. The bloodstain on the front of her pretty dress was spreading like a living thing.

"Will you stay with me until the ambulance comes?"

She was in shock and dying and didn't really know who I was, and I said, "Of course I'll stay. I'm not leaving you."

"Will they be here soon?"

"Yes, very soon."

"And you'll stay with me until they come?"

"Of course."

"You promise?"

"Yes."

She seemed to smile a little at that and then her eyes closed, gently, like a child going to sleep, and her hands fell away from her chest, no longer folded in prayer, and I didn't have to break my promise that I wouldn't leave her. She was already gone.

ABOUT THE AUTHOR

Jonathan Ames is the author of several books, including *Wake Up, Sir!* and, most recently, *A Man Named Doll*. His novels *The Extra Man* and *You Were Never Really Here* have been adapted into films, and he's the creator of two television series, *Blunt Talk* and *Bored to Death*.